THE RABBIT'S UMBRELLA

BY GEORGE PLIMPTON

Illustrated by WILLIAM PÈNE DU BOIS

You wouldn't think there'd be much room under a rabbit's umbrella, except, of course, for the rabbit himself. But beneath the shelter of *The Rabbit's Umbrella* you will find a dog the size of a bear, a woman who couldn't get her Ford in reverse, a policeman incapable of untangling his traffic jams, three timid burglars living in a haunted house, a retired doctor who sees a panda at a tea-party, a streetcar conductor worried about losing his streetcar, a sly pet-shop owner who could sell a one-eyed bullfrog to a customer asking for a Siamese cat, a mother who thought a poodle the most important thing in life, a father who ran through a warm night with his bedroom slippers flapping about his feet, and a boy who finally got the pet he wanted.

You wouldn't think a plot containing such a strange assortment of characters existed. But *The Rabbit's Umbrella*, as large and gay as a circus tent, houses a plot as full of twists and surprises as a troupe of juggling clowns.

And as for the rabbit himself, the umbrella-holder, whether at the close of the book you think him a figment of the imagination, or actually feel him standing behind you watching you read the book, you'll never forget him after having seen him carouse through Mr. Plimpton's lighthearted fantasy.

The Rabbit's Umbrella is peppered with amusing, imaginative illustrations by William Pène du Bois, which are a complete delight in themselves.

THE RABBIT'S UMBRELLA

THE
RABBIT'S UMBRELLA

BY GEORGE PLIMPTON

ILLUSTRATED BY WILLIAM PÈNE DU BOIS

THE VIKING PRESS · NEW YORK

FOR PETER, PATSY, AND LUCAS MATTHIESSEN

29070

THE RABBIT'S UMBRELLA

PROLOGUE

YOUNG BOY SITTING IN LARGE ARMCHAIR: *Well, now that you've finally decided to tell me a story, what sort of people are you going to tell me about? Are the guards from Buckingham Palace in the story, or a long-fingered witch, or perhaps a bear of great size?*

No, I'm afraid not.

YOUNG BOY: *You've included a dwarf, haven't you? And if not, certainly a giant with a large appetite?*

Neither, I'm ashamed to say. The characters in the story you're about to hear include Mr. and Mrs. Henry Montague; their son Peter; a pet-shop owner called Mr. Perkins; Mr. Otway, the streetcar motorman; Mr. Delaney, who is a police officer; and finally, a doctor, Doctor Trimble.

YOUNG BOY: *They don't sound particularly exciting to me. Hadn't you better throw in a monstrous dragon, and a magician or two—the kind with tall pointed hats covered with stars and half moons?*

I'm afraid either a dragon or the kind of magician you speak of would overtax my imagination. But may I hasten to add that other characters in my story that

7

might interest you more include an enormous dog named Lump, three robbers—Pease, Punch, and Mr. Bouncely—a number of shouting parrots, and a rabbit with an umbrella.

YOUNG BOY: *That sounds a bit better. Are the robbers exciting?*

Very exciting indeed.

YOUNG BOY: *Very well then, I should like to hear the story, especially if it takes place in an interesting part of the world—the African jungle perhaps.*

Again I must disappoint you; the story takes place in the town of Adams, somewhere in America, though I never can remember quite where.

YOUNG BOY: *How do we get to this town of Adams if you don't know where it is? We know where Africa is. Hadn't we better go there?*

It's simple enough to get to Adams once you find the station from which the train leaves. You'd have no difficulty in recognizing the train. The locomotive is small, and you'd think it a switch engine if it weren't for the important puffing of its voice as it waits at the head of the baggage car and the two coaches. It has an enormous, tall smokestack; a whistle with a half-moon mouth; and a brass bell—a big one—with a cord running back into the cab for the engineer to pull when the conductor gives his signal to start the train.

9

THE RABBIT'S UMBRELLA

The train takes the trip to Adams twice a day: once in the morning, then again at night. In the daytime the wind coming through the big, open windows is cool and has the smell of flowers and woods. But the train never goes so fast that you can't hear the crickets singing in the ditches or see clearly the flowers by the road-bed. The telegraph poles don't whir by but pass slowly, the swoop of the telephone wires strung between them slow and long. You can stand out on the back platform and watch the silver track come from under you with a great clatter and stretch back into the distance between the trees, which are gusty and show the white of their leaves in the windy passing of the train.

If you took the train at night you would see how the fire under the boilers is reflected on the passing trees in a warm red glow and how the moon shines on the track, and you would hear the locomotive whistle. Its sound is not like the screams from the big Diesels which shriek through the night, frightening the crows roosting in the pine trees, but a pleasant *poop!*—so weak that only the frogs splashing in the long shallow pools alongside the railroad track look up with bulging eyes.

I can't remember whether you get on this train in Chicago, Memphis, New York, or San Francisco, but after an hour out in the country, or maybe two, the conductor opens the door and shouts down the aisle

that the train is coming into Adams. Up front the whistle blows to wake the station master, sleeping in his wicker rocking chair at the little station far ahead.

Now if you look at the map which I've drawn for you at the front of the book, you'll see just where the train is going.

First it comes out of the forest where the owls live, and rattles across the old wooden bridge under which the catfish, waiting for worms to be dropped to them from the end of small boys' fishlines, grow fat in the brown water. Then, after crossing the bridge, the train goes through another stretch of woods where a rabbit with an umbrella lives. Just at the edge of the woods, in a field full of rotting stumps, is the town's haunted house—an old dilapidated building with a sagging roof. Its windows, some of them broken, reflect the light of the sun in the glint of glass eyes. Three people live in

the haunted house, but I shan't tell you who they are
until the proper time.

YOUNG BOY: *The three robbers.*

I'm not going to say until the proper time.

YOUNG BOY: *It's the three robbers! I know it's the
three robbers!*

You'll simply have to wait and see. Now look at the
map again. Up the long hill there, to the right, you can
see the white pillars of the country club where Mr.
Henry Montague has lunch every day. Out in back
there are tennis courts, and in front there's a deep, blue
swimming pool with a turtle at the bottom. We have
only a quick glimpse of the country club from the train
because our view is blocked by the Montague thimble
factory and that freight car standing on a siding, waiting to be filled up with thimbles. The factory is the
largest establishment in Adams, and, as you can see, its
buildings stretch along both sides of the track for quite
some way.

THE RABBIT'S UMBRELLA

As the train comes out past the last factory shed, creeps by the water tower and along the station platform, and passes the baggage master, dozing in his chair, once more the whistle goes *poop!* The baggage master jumps and comes toward the train, smiling sheepishly and rubbing the sleep from his eyes.

We've arrived in Adams. Did you enjoy the train ride?

YOUNG BOY: *Very much. Did you say there was a rabbit with an umbrella living in the wood near the haunted house?*

Yes, I did. But I've decided not to put him in the story.

YOUNG BOY: *Why not? He's got to be in the story. You can't mention a rabbit that has an umbrella without keeping him in the story.*

All right, all right. I'll put him in. I can't think for the life of me why I ever mentioned him.

YOUNG BOY: *Thank you. Thank you very much. Now the story?*

Certainly. It will be a pleasure to get on with it.

ONE

In the old days two streetcars used to run the tracks in Adams, both brightly painted, swaying in their speed through the quiet of the town. Everybody was proud of them, took rides in them, and thought about them when they weren't taking rides. They thought how pleasant the spring air was as it came through the big windows; and how you could look down from so high above the street that you could see the tops of people's heads; and how you could read the advertisements tacked to the curve of the ceiling, or watch the driver work the controls, or merely close your eyes and sit on the slatted seats, listening to the clatter of the wheels and the big bell clanging overhead.

But after a while the townspeople of Adams began to think about something else. They began to think about thimbles.

For in Mr. Montague's factory thimbles were made, hundreds of them a day, packed in freight cars, and shipped off to be sold. The Montague thimble was a good thimble—as fine as any thimble in the country—and if you took the time to inspect each of the little silver hats perched on a million third fingers of the nation's seamstresses, you would find that most of them were Montague thimbles. In no time at all the town of Adams became the thimble capital of the world, and its people found themselves rich.

Mr. Montague bought a Cadillac for himself and his wife, and he bought his son Peter a little one-seater, with pedals to push to make it go. Mrs. Phipps, who lives up toward the country club, bought herself a Ford that she never really learned to back properly and a black poodle named Rasputin. She went ahead and planted a rose garden behind her house, something she'd talked about doing for twenty years. Mr. Perkins, the pet-shop owner, ordered four parrots, and on the sign which hung outside the shop's entrance he

replaced the missing Ps, so the sign read PERKINS' PET SHOP and not ERKINS' ET SHO. Dr. Trimble bought a tall black hat; Officer Delaney purchased a new whistle, complete with chain; and Mr. Finch, the night watchman at the factory, made enough money to buy himself a watch with a luminous dial, so he didn't have to strike a match in the dark of night to see what time it was.

THE RABBIT'S UMBRELLA

Naturally, with the people of Adams driving around in the things they'd bought—or planting them—and thinking about what else they were going to buy, there wasn't enough time to remember about the two streetcars and certainly no time to waste in riding in them.

So the streetcars fell into disrepair. The bright crimson of their painted sides was weatherbeaten into old-barn red, the windows were stained and didn't go up and down properly, the big bell had a rusty sound to it, and the only passengers were small boys and their dogs. The streetcars moved very slowly through the town, rearing above the crush of traffic like old houses toppled from river banks and caught in the grip of a log jam. The streetcars were hopelessly inefficient, and, sure enough, one day one of them (on the recommendation of the mayor's council) was sold to a restaurateur named Harry Myers and moved down to the highway. Here it was installed as a Harry's Diner. Its wheels removed, it rested in a gravel parking lot, surrounded by big continental trucks whose drivers sat in the diner, drinking coffee and talking incessantly, as if to make up for the quiet hours of the long miles of their trucking routes.

Mr. Otway, the motorman of the one remaining streetcar, was fond of saying that late at night when he drove the streetcar up into the hills and pulled at the

bellcord, the town quiet and asleep below, a plaintive
echo of the bell would return from the direction of
Harry's Diner—as if that old streetcar, now freshly
painted a bright yellow, and warm inside, with the rich
smoke of hamburgers coming from the tin chimney in
its roof, would like to tear from its foundations and run
through the deserted streets, through the forests and
up the hills, and feel against its painted sides the cool
winds of night.

THE RABBIT'S UMBRELLA

But Mr. Otway's nice sentiment is not something that mayors' councils understand. The councilmen of Adams felt strongly that even one streetcar was uneconomical: it cluttered up the streets and caused traffic jams; it was an ugly thing to have running around anyway; and it would serve the town better set up as another Harry's Diner on the opposite side of town. Every Saturday morning the mayor's council discussed the matter in the town hall, and every Saturday morning it was more obvious that the councilmen had forgotten how important to their youth were the streetcar's big bell, the clatter of its wheels, and the open windows with the spring air coming in and so high above the street that you could look down and see the tops of people's heads.

Three people in Adams, though, felt strongly about the streetcar and shuddered every Saturday morning when they knew the mayor's council was in session. I'm not talking about small boys and their dogs, who would have been concerned if they weren't so busy feeding catfish from bent-hairpin hooks and climbing haystacks. I'm talking about Mr. Otway, Officer Delaney, and Dr. Trimble.

Mr. Otway was the driver of the streetcar. He was also responsible for a complicated box, set alongside his seat, that registered the dimes and nickels dropped

in by the passengers but didn't register the hatpins, the fishhooks, and the small pebbles which were dropped in, sometimes by mistake and sometimes on purpose. Whichever was the case, the electric motor in the box stopped in confusion, and Mr. Otway would then have to scratch around inside and extract whatever was causing the trouble, and more often than not hand the hatpin, the fishhook, or the pebble back to its owner. If the owner happened to be a very small boy with a large dog beside him, Mr. Otway would hand the article back and say, "Now don't go stuffing things like that in my box," and the boy would take the fishhook, or whatever it was, and go back to the end of the streetcar, sit down quietly with his dog, and look out the window. Mr. Otway was a sad-looking man with a long face. When the

21

streetcar was caught in a traffic jam, which it usually was, except at night, Mr. Otway would prop up his newspaper on the fare box, occasionally reaching up to pull rather hopelessly at the bellcord, without lifting his eyes from his paper. Mr. Otway loved the streetcar passionately.

So did Officer Delaney. He used to try to direct the streetcar through the market-day traffic jams, but it wasn't much use. He stood in a white traffic box in the middle of the honking confusion, a large man with a face that flushed purple when he was angry. On marketing days he was usually angry. "Mrs. Phipps!" he'd shout, the veins in his neck standing out. "Get that Ford outa there. Back it up!"

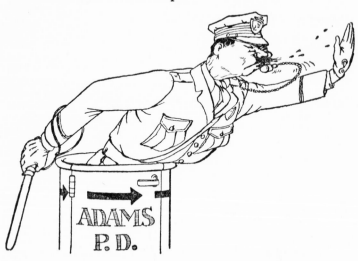

THE RABBIT'S UMBRELLA

Mrs. Phipps, a tidy, gray-haired woman who owned the biggest rose garden in Adams but who had the greatest difficulty in putting her car in reverse, would wrestle desperately with the gearshift and announce shrilly, "Oh, ye gods and little fishes, officer, I simply can't."

Officer Delaney would then blow a terrible blast on his whistle, leave his white traffic box, stalk through the traffic jam right past Mrs. Phipps's Ford without so much as a how-de-do, and stride into Mr. Tompkins' drugstore to have a ginger ale to soothe his nerves.

A great, brooding man, he'd sit on the tall counter stool, inattentive to the confusion outside, and peer into his glass, watching the little bubbles rise up in straight, even lines, never bumping or jostling one another. "Now, why doesn't traffic behave as well?" he'd ask the bubbles that popped on the liquid's surface.

Sometimes he'd talk to Mr. Tompkins about the good old days in his traffic box when all he had to worry about in the square were a few horse and buggies, the two streetcars of course, and old Mrs. Jenkins' electric car, which used to get out of control every month or so and revolve in tight circles like a dog chasing its tail.

But now— With a shake of his head he'd lay the money for his ginger ale on the counter, nod to Mr. Tompkins, and march out into the square, where for the twentieth time he'd show Mrs. Phipps how to put her Ford in reverse. Then with a great blast of his whistle he'd start the traffic inching around his white box.

Every night after dinner Officer Delaney walked down to the town square and climbed aboard the streetcar where Mr. Otway and Dr. Trimble waited for him, and off they would go into the evening, sometimes not returning to the square until well after midnight.

The three took turns sitting in the driver's seat and working the controls. Dr. Trimble especially enjoyed driving the streetcar. As he did so he imagined himself the captain of a clipper ship. "Cast off the hawsers!" he would shout in his rumbling bass as the streetcar began to inch forward. At the approach of a curve he would call out, "Stand by to go on the port tack!" and at the curve itself, "Port your helm!" while behind him Mr. Otway, his face as solemn as a deacon's, and Officer Delaney, blowing his whistle, would rush around among the wooden seats, pretending to do the things one does when porting one's helm.

Dr. Trimble wore a tall black hat, and under thick eyebrows his blue eyes sparkled like the sea. He had been all over the world and had done many strange and wonderful things, such as riding yaks and touching the bones certain people like to wear through their noses; and he knew how far camels can spit; and he had

danced by the light of Japanese lanterns on Chinese junks—in fact, there were few things Dr. Trimble hadn't seen and done.

He still saw remarkable things. Every night or so during the streetcar rides he would suddenly point out the window and shout, "Look! Look there, three points off the starboard bow." Officer Delaney and Mr. Otway would rush to the window and look out, but they never saw anything but the big squares of yellow light on the shrubbery outside, or the trees, or the picket gates, or whatever it was the streetcar was passing at the time, and they would say, "What, Dr. Trimble, was it?"

And Dr. Trimble would slap his thigh and answer, "Why, it was that rabbit, it was that rabbit with the umbrella." Officer Delaney and Mr. Otway would look quickly again, but there would be nothing there but the quiet night and the big yellow squares of light moving along beside them.

Very late at night on their way back to the town square the three men would discuss the future of the streetcar—very gloomily too, for there seemed no hope of persuading the mayor's council that the town needed a streetcar. They had tried a petition, but not many people had signed it. The townspeople said that they were too busy, that the streetcar tracks swerved their cars so they seemed to be driving on ice, and that they were

THE RABBIT'S UMBRELLA

held up in traffic jams behind the streetcar and made late for important appointments.

"There seems no hope," said Mr. Otway.

"We'll have to trust in a miracle," said Officer Delaney.

"Perhaps, then," said Dr. Trimble, looking out in the darkness, "he'll come to help us."

"Who?" asked Officer Delaney and Mr. Otway.

"Why, the rabbit, of course," replied Dr. Trimble. "The rabbit with the umbrella."

TWO

YOUNG BOY SITTING IN LARGE ARMCHAIR: *Is this the end of a chapter?*

Not really; the end of the chapter is one page back. This is the *beginning* of a chapter, and you must be very quiet.

YOUNG BOY: *I'm very curious about one thing. I'm curious about that rabbit Doctor Trimble sees from the streetcar windows, the one with the umbrella. If he's going to save the streetcar he's a very important character indeed, and I don't see how you can leave him out of the story, which you said you were going to do back in the prologue.*

I didn't say the rabbit with the umbrella was going to save the streetcar. I didn't even suggest that the streetcar was going to be saved. I continue to say, however, that the rabbit with the umbrella is a very difficult character and I wish I hadn't mentioned him.

If I may—that is, if you will let me—continue, I should like to forget the streetcar for a while, and Mr. Otway, Officer Delaney, Doctor Trimble, and especially that rabbit. I should like to tell you, if you'll let me, about Mr. Montague's son Peter, and the pet he wanted.

YOUNG BOY: *Why, certainly, though that rabbit—* Thank you.

Now Peter Montague, aged nine, owned the smallest vehicle in Adams—larger perhaps than one of the wheels of Mr. Otway's streetcar, but not much. It was a car without a motor but with pedals to push, and so small that Officer Delaney's heart would have skipped with delight. For Peter's little car could have navigated through the traffic jam downtown with the greatest of ease, dodging in and around cars, even underneath them. Peter, being nine, wasn't allowed to take his car down to Officer Delaney's traffic jam; he could drive his car only as far as the front gate of the big garden around the Montague house. So he attached carts at its end to make a train, and he pedaled up and down the garden paths and through the house, calling out, "Beep! beep!" as he went. When he wasn't calling out, "Beep! beep!" he made a noise, supposed to represent the motor of his little car, by rapidly vibrating his tongue, producing a sound known in some circles as a Bronx cheer. His father found it particularly disturbing, especially when he was trying to work in his library,

William Pène du Bois

and he told his son so. "Don't make that noise with your tongue, Peter; it's most disagreeable."

"But Father," said Peter, "it's my car's motor. You can't have a car without a motor, can you, Father?"

Well, there wasn't much Mr. Montague could say to *that*, so he didn't.

But even with his little car to amuse him, Peter was unhappy. He wasn't unhappy, as was Mr. Otway, the streetcar motorman, because he thought his vehicle was going to be taken away from him but because, although he had all sorts of toys—a doll's house with an elevator that was operated by turning a handle in the roof, a large elephant on wheels with a ring in his back that made a squeak when pulled, a baseball bat, and so forth—what he wanted more than anything else he didn't have. That was a pet. He liked his elephant, but he wanted an animal without wheels on its feet.

So one Saturday morning after he'd finished breakfast, Peter stepped into his car and started to pedal down the hall to his father's study. As he went he thought what sort of pet he'd ask for—a dog, for instance; a cat, or a parrot perhaps; or maybe a turtle. But he dismissed parrots and turtles immediately. Parrots are liable to snap and aren't as good talkers as they're made out to be; turtles scratch across the linoleum floors of kitchens, and there's not much else they can do except eat leaves. It occurred to Peter that cats, although worthy of more consideration, are complicated animals—mysterious, and usually difficult to get along with, smiling all the time, their mouths fixed in a steady smirk beneath their solemn eyes, smirking even when there isn't anything particularly funny to see. It's almost impossible to tell what's going on in a cat's mind, except when dinnertime approaches and he rubs his back along your trouser leg and purrs like distant summer thunder.

Now dogs, Peter decided as he pedaled through the door of his father's study, are simple animals. When they feel miserable they hump themselves up like pieces of wet paper and *look* miserable, and when they laugh they run their tongues out and laugh hard, the laughter showing in their brown eyes.

So when Peter had parked his car by Mr. Montague's desk he pushed the black button on the steering wheel, called out, "Beep! beep!" to attract attention, and followed that with, "Father, I want a dog. I've decided I want a dog."

Mr. Montague looked up from his desk. "What's that, son?" he asked.

"I would like a pet, Father. A dog," replied Peter.

Mr. Montague leaned back in his swivel chair. "Well, now, I don't know, son," he said.

"You don't know what, Father?"

"Peter, please stop that noise." Peter's tongue was vibrating at full speed as he moved his car slightly forward. "I can't hear myself think."

Peter stopped the motor noise and repeated, "Please, Father. I want a dog for my own."

"But, Peter, that's a big responsibility, and a big present as well. Hadn't you better wait until your birthday? Then we'll discuss it again." Mr. Montague leaned forward in the swivel chair.

"But Father," said Peter, "my birthday is seven months away, and by that time I may not *want* a dog."

The swivel chair creaked again and Mr. Montague sighed deeply. Suddenly, however, he remembered that his wife, Harriet, disliked dogs. She kept a neat house and lived in dread of seeing a trail of muddy paw marks across the polished floors and of discovering old bones under chairs or tufts of dog hair on her sofas. So Mr. Montague said to his son, "You go and ask your mother, Peter. If she says you can have a dog, I'll go downtown and get you one. I'll even do it this morning, but first you must get your mother's permission."

"Thank you, Father," said the boy confidently.

Mr. Montague watched his son back up the car, wheel it around, and pedal off toward the living room, where Mrs. Montague spent her mornings arranging flowers in big vases. His son almost always got the best of him, but this time, by golly, Mr. Montague believed he'd fixed Peter good and proper.

Well, how was Mr. Montague to know that his wife had had a sudden change of opinion about dogs?

Two days before, at a tea party in Mrs. Phipps's rose garden, Mrs. Montague had been approached by Mrs. Phipps's black miniature poodle, Rasputin, who pranced up to her on his clipped toes and to whom she quite lost her heart. The poodle singled her out to beg a piece of toast from; he sat up on his hind legs and looked her straight in the eye with such a human, meaningful expression that Mrs. Montague overcame her fear that her fingers would be snapped off and gingerly offered him a canapé. Rasputin took it with such delicacy (not a crumb dropped on the green lawn) that Mrs. Montague decided she approved of such dogs—more so perhaps than she did of some of her own friends at Mrs. Phipps's party—so she fed the poodle another canapé, two pieces of toast, and a stuffed egg, all of which disappeared quickly. When she overheard guests telling Mrs. Phipps how "divine" and how "charming" they thought Rasputin, Mrs. Montague suddenly turned jealous. How nice it would be, she thought, to have a dog like Rasputin bouncing around, eating canapés on *her* lawn at *her* tea parties. And so she resolved right

then and there, as she fed Rasputin a bit of an éclair, to speak to Mr. Montague the first chance she had.

She would call the poodle a fine and distinguished name, and as she clipped and snipped away among the tiger lilies in the living room the name came to her. Minnehaha. Minnehaha, that's what she'd call the dog, and, when she thought of her guests calling out how charming they thought Minnehaha was, her gardening shears got quite out of hand and tiger lily heads dropped and decorated the floor about her feet.

When Peter parked his car beside her and beeped to attract attention and explained that he wanted a dog for a pet and needed her permission, Mrs. Montague snapped her gardening shears shut and said, "Peter, of course you have my permission. We've needed Minnehaha—a dog in this house for the longest time. We'll go and see your father about it right away."

Mr. Montague was thunderstruck. He pushed back his swivel chair and stood up. "Great Scott, Harriet!" he cried. "Have you gone mad?"

"Not at all, Henry," said his wife calmly.

"Father," said Peter excitedly, "you said you'd go right downtown and get a dog if Mother gave her permission. And she has."

"Great Scott!" exclaimed Mr. Montague again.

"You'd better go right down to Mr. Perkins' pet shop, Henry, and pick one out," said his wife. She was having a tea party that very afternoon, and when she realized that Minnehaha would be prancing about among her guests she became quite overcome with excitement. "Quick, Henry!" she said, clicking the gardening shears sharply. "Off you go and get us a dog. I think a poodle, a black one, would be nice—don't you think, Peter?"

"I just want a dog," said Peter, who wasn't quite sure what a poodle was.

36

"That's settled, then," said Mrs. Montague. "A lovely black poodle for Peter."

"Great Scott!" said Mr. Montague for the third time. He walked wearily into the hall to find his hat. "All right, all right," he said.

"Mother, who is Great Scott?" he heard his son ask.

"I don't know, dear. You'll have to ask your father."

"Father, who is—" But Mr. Montague closed the front door quickly and stepped down the garden walk with long strides, glancing nervously over his shoulder.

When he'd passed the garden gate he decided to walk down the driveway to Willow Street and take the streetcar, something he hadn't done for years. Luckily, as he reached the foot of the driveway the streetcar came rattling down the street under the willow trees, shreds of shadow flowing off its roof like running water. The streetcar stopped opposite him with a squeal of brakes and stood quiet, dappled by the sunlight. Mr. Montague stepped aboard.

"Well, Mr. Montague," said Mr. Otway, alone in the car at the controls, "we haven't had you aboard for a long time."

"I'm afraid not, Mr. Otway," replied Mr. Montague. "I just seem to be too busy." He sat down behind the driver's stool. The doors hissed shut and the streetcar started down the hill toward the center of town.

THE RABBIT'S UMBRELLA

Mr. Otway's face was as long as a telephone pole. "This may be the last ride you'll ever take on the old streetcar," he said gloomily over his shoulder. "The mayor's council is meeting today to decide its future. They're going to vote, I hear, and I'm afraid that fellow Harry Myers is going to get himself another diner."

"I'm very sorry to hear that," said Mr. Montague.

"Doctor Trimble is terribly disturbed about it," Mr. Otway continued. "He's so bothered in the head that he says a rabbit with an umbrella is coming to save the streetcar. Now isn't that something, Mr. Montague?" he asked.

"My goodness, it certainly is," agreed Mr. Montague.

"And wouldn't it be something if a rabbit with an umbrella stomped right into that council meeting and made a speech, a real speech?" said Mr. Otway. "But I don't suppose one should put much stock in what the old doctor says, should one, Mr. Montague?"

"Oh, I think so," Mr. Montague assured him. "The doctor's an extraordinary man."

"He is indeed," admitted Mr. Otway, applying the brakes as the streetcar tracks dipped steeply toward the town. "Well, Mr. Montague," he said more brightly, "what brings you down into town this morning?"

"Choosing a dog for my son Peter," replied Mr. Montague. "I'm going down to Mr. Perkins' pet shop to pick one out."

"And what breed do you fancy?" asked Mr. Otway.

"My wife fancies a poodle," Mr. Montague said. "I haven't decided yet."

"Don't care much for them small dogs," Mr. Otway said. "Too much a woman's dog, all scissored up the way they are, bells at their throats, and ribbons on their tails. Give me a dog with fleas on him and burrs in his coat, and big enough so's when you walk through the woods with him you're not scared you're going to lose him under a leaf."

"Perhaps you're right," said Mr. Montague, leaning

39

back against the wooden slats of his seat and peering out the windows. He closed his eyes and tried to remember the dogs of his youth—some of them small dogs with the quick, bright faces of squirrels; others the larger dogs that Mr. Otway preferred, Irish setters that lay before log fires in winter, their toes twitching as they dreamed of rabbits jumping from the brambles. But the more he thought, the less he could make up his mind as to what sort of dog to buy Peter, and he found himself thinking of other things—that he wanted a new hat, that the front lawn needed mowing, what fun it would be to learn to fly an airplane, and other such thoughts that are rocked into one's mind by the motion of a big streetcar.

Suddenly his thoughts were interrupted by Mr. Otway. "We're coming into Officer Delaney's traffic jam," the motorman said. "If you want to get to the Perkins pet shop quickly, you'd better get off an' walk, Mr. Montague. We'll be a long time getting through."

Mr. Montague looked out the window and, sure enough, there was Officer Delaney's red face, shining like a beacon above the roofs of the honking automobiles. "I'll wait, thank you, Mr. Otway," said Mr. Montague. "I haven't decided yet."

Mr. Otway nodded. When he'd stopped the streetcar on the fringe of the traffic jam, he picked up his newspaper, propped it on the fare box, and started to read. Occasionally, without looking up from his paper, he pulled at the bellcord.

Mr. Montague again concentrated on dogs. To his annoyance, the only dog that appeared vividly in his mind was not actually a dog, not a flesh-and-blood dog at any rate, but an iron dog—an iron statue of a dog which stood on a pedestal in the dining room of the country club. The statue was of a long-bodied, crouched dog stalking something in the next room, his nose low to the ground and eager, and a long tail, stiff with excitement, stretched behind him. The something he was stalking was an iron deer in the library, poised for flight, looking back over its gleaming metal shoulder into the dining room at the creeping dog. Sometimes the door between the two rooms was closed; but the dog went right on snuffling at the ground and the deer kept looking back nervously over its shoulder. They had been doing that for fifteen years, ever since Mr. Montague's father had donated the two statues to the country club. Mr. Montague liked the deer well enough, but he didn't spend as much time in the library as he did in eating his countless luncheons in the dining room, so he preferred the low, long-tailed dog, creeping, without so much as a flicker of interest in anything but the iron deer in the library, through a dining room that resounded with

41

the clatter of forks and smelled richly of roast beef.

When the streetcar had finally crawled through Officer Delaney's traffic jam, Mr. Montague stepped off, still unable to chase the iron dog from his mind. As he pushed open the door of Mr. Perkins' pet shop a small camel bell tinkled overhead and a parrot said, "Well, well, well." Mr. Montague walked straight to the counter. The pet shop smelled of goldfish food and straw and parrot perches and white mice.

Mr. Perkins appeared from the back of the shop, his eyes sparkling behind thick spectacles. "Yes, sir?" he asked.

Mr. Montague put his hands on the counter and, looking at the parrot swinging on his perch, he cleared his throat and said, "I would like a large dog with an extremely long tail."

THREE

Mr. Perkins looked up from the counter. "I have just what you're looking for, sir," he said, rubbing his hands together—at first very briskly but then more and more slowly, until they were quiet, as if clasped in prayer. A quizzical look crossed his face and after a pause he asked, "Now, again, sir, just what was it you wanted?"

"A long dog with a long tail," repeated Mr. Montague.

"Ah, of course," said Mr. Perkins. "I have just such a dog. A very special breed indeed." He skipped out from behind the counter. "If you'll just follow me, sir. I keep him out in the garden, where I show him only to my most special customers. This way, sir."

Mr. Perkins was the best salesman in Adams County, so good that he often convinced customers that what they really wanted was not a canary or a goldfish or a parrot, but a one-eyed cat, or a bullfrog, or perhaps a pink-eyed white mouse—whatever pet, in fact, Mr. Perkins was having difficulty in selling. He sold twenty-five guinea pigs to a Mrs. Blackstone who came in to buy a Siamese cat. To a Mrs. Howard who wanted to buy a canary for her aging aunt he managed to sell a big snapping turtle at an exorbitant price, throwing in a garter snake for good measure.

But there was one pet in Mr. Perkins' pet shop which even he, try as he would, was unable to sell. So when Mr. Montague said, "I want a long dog with a long tail," Mr. Perkins practically jumped over the counter in his excitement. For his unsalable pet was a dog, a very large dog with a sweeping tail, and nearly as long in body as was Mr. Perkins himself.

"Certainly, certainly, sir. I have just the dog you're looking for!" shouted Mr. Perkins as he guided Mr. Montague through the back of his shop.

The dog Mr. Perkins had in mind had arrived in a basket with seven other puppies on a cold night of the previous winter. Puppies, small turtles, bullfrogs, and other pets were often left on Mr. Perkins' doorstep by families who already had enough puppies, small turtles, and so forth in their homes, for it was known that Mr. Perkins would take good care of these pets. And Mr. Perkins did. He kept them in clean cages, groomed them, and sold them at a handsome profit.

Take the eight puppies which had arrived that winter, for example. Seven of them grew up to become splendid-looking dogs—Irish setters, with just a pinch

44

of chow and a dash of spaniel. Mr. Perkins had had no trouble in selling them into families who had large yards for them to play in and log fires for them to lie in front of during the winter months.

But the eighth was quite another matter. He became the living nightmare of Mr. Perkins' life! He caused Mr. Perkins to cry out suddenly in public places, such as church, and so confused the pet-shop owner that he fed his parrots carrots, his rabbits birdseed, and his gold-fish dog biscuits. For, though this eighth dog started out to look more like a spaniel than the others—a small, reasonable dog—suddenly he grew to the size of an Irish setter, then twice the size, then ballooned out three times as bulky as a large chow, and finally to such a size that he crowded out the other dogs and filled the front show window of the shop like a cat-fish in a drinking glass. Mr. Perkins had to build him a special cage out in the back yard. Here the great dog sat—as large, when he finally stopped growing, as a sofa—a gray, shaggy, unmade bed of a dog, with a long bush of a tail that crashed against the slats of the pen when Mr. Perkins brought him his dinner. He had big sad eyes the size of saucers, enormous drooping ears like a tired elephant's; and he sat quietly in his cage, soundless, as if ashamed of his size.

Mr. Perkins tried all his tricks of salesmanship, but

when he took customers out to the pen in the back yard they told him curtly, "Mr. Perkins, we're not in the market for a dog that looks like a bear."

So Mr. Perkins, unscrupulous as ever, wrote to a zoo in Chicago and said he had a well-behaved brown bear for sale. But the zoo man came and said, "That's not a bear you have there, Mr. Perkins. That's a dog that looks like a moose, and we're overloaded with moose at our zoo. Sorry."

It seemed as if there were nothing to be done. The furrow in Mr. Perkins' brow deepened and his voice grew soft and moody. But when he had guided Mr. Montague into his back garden and the two stood in front of the dog's enormous pen, you wouldn't have known Mr. Perkins had a problem in the world. "Now regard that marvelous specimen of dog, sir!" he cried, his voice rich with pride. "Best dog I have."

"Great Scott," said Mr. Montague, looking up into the dog's face. "He's a very large dog, isn't he?"

"Some might call him large, some small," replied Mr. Perkins. "It's a matter of opinion."

"He seems very large to me," said Mr. Montague. "What sort of dog is he?"

"What breed of dog were you looking for?" asked Mr. Perkins craftily.

"Well, my wife fancies a poodle."

46

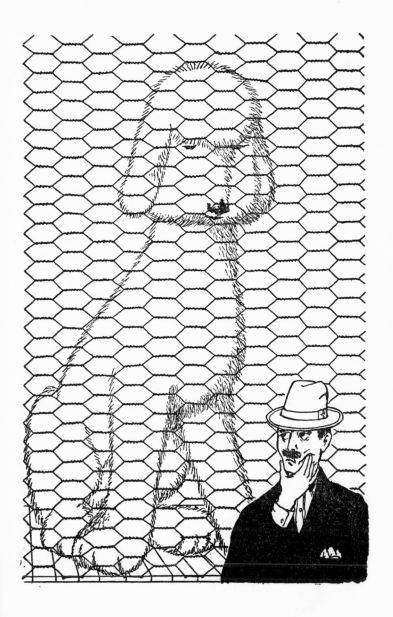

"Very likely," shouted Mr. Perkins frantically. "Perfectly possible this dog is one of the largest and rarest poodles in the world."

"Well," said Mr. Montague doubtfully, "I don't know. Have you got any other dogs I could look at?"

"Not that I know of," said Mr. Perkins—which wasn't quite the truth, for a yapping suddenly rose from the kennels at the other end of the garden. Mr. Montague looked at Mr. Perkins. "Bullfinches," explained Mr. Perkins; that was the only word that popped to his mind immediately. "A flock of them," he added, turning up the palms of his hands.

Mr. Montague would have raised an eyebrow, but at that moment the dog stood up and started to wag his long tail, slowly at first, then so hard that the pen shook under the blows. Mr. Perkins ran toward the dog, shouting, "Help! He's breaking out!" while he strained against the pen to keep it from coming apart. But Mr. Montague offered no assistance. He looked into the dog's saucer-sized eyes and saw there the loneliness and the need for the friendship of a boy; and the wish to run free in meadows of corn, to investigate back alleys and garbage cans, and to lie in front of winter fires, feeling the warmth against his thick coat; and other things important to a dog, no matter of what size. So Mr. Montague suddenly made up his mind and said,

48

"All right, Mr. Perkins, I've decided to buy this dog. He'll be just the dog for my boy, Peter."

Mr. Perkins, still straining against the pen, gave a little shriek and slumped to his knees. "Mercy!" he whispered.

"I'll buy the dog," repeated Mr. Montague. "I'd like to take him home with me right now."

"Certainly, sir," Mr. Perkins said weakly, and, stumbling to his feet, he worked the lock free and opened the door of the pen. The dog snuffled and stepped gingerly out into the garden.

"How much do I owe you for him?" asked Mr. Montague.

Usually at this question Mr. Perkins' eyes would sparkle and he would say, "Well, now, I don't know. This is a mighty, mighty valuable specimen, but I'll make you a bargain if you buy one or two of my parrots and a garter snake." But this time Mr. Perkins said, "Five dollars," and even after he was paid he was too flustered to think properly. "Shall I wrap him for you?" he asked.

"No, thank you," replied Mr. Montague smiling. "I'll take him home with me as he is."

Unfortunately, getting the dog home was easier said than done, as Mr. Montague soon discovered. The great dog had never been in the outside world before.

His eyes were large and deep and a little frightened; he put each paw down as if the earth were covered with tiny flakes of glass; he began to snuffle. "Come along now, dog," called Mr. Montague, plucking his finger in the air and smiling encouragingly. But the dog wouldn't budge. It was only with the greatest difficulty and pushing and heaving and yelling directions to each other that Mr. Montague and Mr. Perkins managed to get him through the pet shop, where the parrots were frantic on their perches, and shouting, and in their bowls the goldfish round-mouthed with surprise. Above the front door of the shop the camel's bell pealed ceaselessly as they inched the dog through, Mr. Montague outside on the street, tugging at the dog's collar, his feet braced against the side of the building; and, inside his shop, Mr. Perkins pushing at the dog from the rear, shouting, "Hy'ar! hy'ar!" like a farmer calling his mules.

Once on the pavement, the dog took one look at the honking confusion of Officer Delaney's traffic jam and set his feet so firmly and looked so large and unmovable, that after a few tentative pushes Mr. Perkins took a large bandanna handkerchief from his pocket, mopped his brow, and told Mr. Montague there wasn't anything else *he* could do, and besides it was time he fed his goldfish. So Mr. Perkins returned to his shop, the camel bell tinkling over the door as it closed behind him, and Mr. Montague was left alone on the street with the dog.

He rested a moment; then, with his hands on the dog's collar, he pulled strenuously, grunting with the effort, as the dog's neck stretched like a piece of rubber. So Mr. Montague walked around and pushed at the dog from the rear, but although the dog's rump rose up in the air like a jacked-up car he still would not budge. "Oh, get along with you," muttered Mr. Montague, feeling hot and uncomfortable.

Finally he decided there was only one thing he could do and that was to *carry* the dog out to one of the town taxis and have him driven home. So, struggling like a furniture-mover heaving up the bulk of a large carpet, Mr. Montague lifted the dog into the air and draped him about his neck. With the dog's tail brushing the ground on one side while his nose, snuffling again, scraped against the pavement on the other, Mr. Montague, his body bent by the weight of this enormous neckpiece, his hat crushed down over his eyes, tottered out into Officer Delaney's traffic jam to find a taxi.

Officer Delaney took one look at this newest addition to his traffic jam, blew a terrible blast on his whistle, and stalked into Mr. Tompkins' drugstore to have his soothing ginger ale. "There's a fellow out there in my traffic jam carrying around a caribou," he told Mr. Tompkins, who was standing behind the counter. "I simply don't know what the world is coming to." Unbelieving, Mr. Tompkins hung his polishing rag on the water spigot and went to the door. Sure enough, he saw a man bent practically to the knees, staggering from taxi to taxi with a huge animal draped about his shoulders. So Mr. Tompkins returned to the counter, and *he* had a ginger ale.

I'm not saying that Mr. Montague couldn't have done with a ginger ale as well. Not a taxi was to be found

that would accept him or his cargo. "No, mister," the taxi drivers said. "Can't allow you in the car with that animal you've got there. Sorry, mister."

Just as his knees were about to buckle, Mr. Montague saw from under the brim of his crushed-down hat the streetcar standing just where he had left it, as big and motionless as a house. He hunched his shoulders, trying to jiggle the dog into a more comfortable position on his back, and set out through the maze of trucks and cars for the streetcar.

Seeing him approach, Mr. Otway put down his paper, and between the two of them they pushed and hauled the dog aboard and settled him on one of the wooden seats.

"My goodness, Mr. Montague," the motorman said. "You've bought yourself one big armful of dog."

Mr. Montague mopped his brow with a handkerchief. "I certainly have, haven't I?" he replied, staring at the dog as if seeing it for the first time.

"What breed of dog is it?" asked Mr. Otway.

"Mr. Perkins tells me it's probably a very large poodle."

Mr. Otway looked at the dog for a long time, then at Mr. Montague. "Well, it's a very large dog at any rate," he agreed, and he walked down to the controls at the other end of the streetcar. "I'll take you up Willow

54

Street," he said. "There's no sense my finishing the run
down to the railroad station. You're my only passenger
of the day."

"That would be very kind," said Mr. Montague,
sitting down in a seat in front of the dog.

The streetcar crept out of the traffic jam and started
back up the hill toward the Montague house. Mr.
Montague stared out the window, breathing heavily
from his exertions, feeling the wind against his face,
comforting and cool. In back of him the dog rested
quietly, looking to Mr. Montague like a man hunched
forward in his seat and bundled to his ears in a heavy
raccoon coat.

After a moment of silence Mr. Otway turned from

the controls and said sadly, "Well, Mr. Montague, while you were in the pet shop, old Smitty, the janitor in the town hall, came out to tell me the results of the mayor's committee meeting on the future of the old streetcar here."

Mr. Montague looked up.

"Mr. Myers has won himself a new restaurant," Mr. Otway said bitterly. "The committee voted that in a week or so the old streetcar here be sold to him. He'll move it down to the east side of town and set it up on Highway Ten as a diner."

"I'm very sorry to hear that," Mr. Montague said. "I wish I could do something about it."

"I don't know how I'm going to break the news to Officer Delaney and the good Doctor Trimble. They'll be heartbroken, but there's nothing to be done I'm afraid," said Mr. Otway, staring up the long, willow-arched hill. "It's very sad." He patted the big brake at his side. "Doctor Trimble's rabbit with the umbrella never showed up, did he?"

"I'm very sorry," Mr. Montague said again.

Well, when the streetcar reached the foot of the long driveway Mr. Otway and Mr. Montague lifted the dog from his wooden seat, and between them they carried him down the steps and set him on the ground. "Do you think he's going to go?" asked Mr. Otway.

"I hope so," said Mr. Montague. He knelt before the dog and looked into his solemn eyes. "We're almost home," he said. "Now up you go, and let's walk the rest of the way." Mr. Montague jumped to his feet and to set a good example he set off briskly up the driveway. He snapped his fingers, calling out, "Come along now, come along now." But after a short distance he turned back to look, and there was Mr. Otway, standing just where he had been before, and beside him, with his pink tongue dangling from his mouth, was the dog, still motionless.

"He's laughing his head off at you," Mr. Otway called up the hill. "It doesn't look as though he's going to go at all."

Mr. Montague strode back down the hill angrily. But when he stood next to the dog and saw how very big the dog was, his anger turned to despair and he said hopelessly, "What, Mr. Otway, are we going to do? I'm too worn out to carry him a foot farther."

Mr. Otway scratched his long chin. "We might try pushing him up the driveway," he suggested. "Might be that he'll roll along nice and easy."

"Well, let's try it," said Mr. Montague. Together they set their shoulders to the dog's back and pushed. At first their feet slipped in the gravel, but after a while the dog started to scrape along the driveway. Finally

57

they got him going quite nicely, the gravel curling over
his toes and away from his haunches like bow waves;
and behind them, stretching down the driveway like a
ship's wake, was the smooth track of their passing.

58

THE RABBIT'S UMBRELLA

"We're almost there," puffed Mr. Otway.

"Pffff," hissed Mr. Montague, raising up and looking over the dog's shoulder and seeing the gate and, behind, his house and the big elm tree. "We're here," he said, and he sat down suddenly in the driveway. Mr. Otway sat down too, his head resting against the dog's back, and the two puffed for a while until Mr. Otway said he had to be getting back to his streetcar. Mr. Montague thanked him and told him how sorry he was about the mayor's council's decision, how he hoped everything would work out somehow. He watched Mr. Otway walk down the driveway, one hand on his hip, his legs bent slightly, as if Mr. Otway had spent his day moving pianos.

Then Mr. Montague stood up. "Come along, you," he said rather hopelessly. To his surprise the dog stood up and shook himself until he was completely surrounded by a thick cloud of driveway dust. Mr. Montague squeaked open the front gate. "Come along," he said again.

Mrs. Montague and Peter were waiting on the front steps. The warm smile of greeting that Mrs. Montague had reserved for her Minnehaha vanished as the dog entered the garden, and she shouted at her husband, "Oh, Henry, that's *not* a poodle. How could you?"

"Mr. Perkins says it's probably a very large type of

poodle," said Mr. Montague defensively but absent-mindedly from the gate: he was watching Peter for the boy's reaction to his new pet. And he smiled happily for the first time that morning as Peter jumped like a summer grasshopper, ran across the garden, and put his arms around the dog's neck. And Mr. Montague smiled more broadly still when he heard Peter say, "He's a wonderful big lump of a dog. I shall call him Lump." And Mr. Montague's smile broke into laughter that sounded like a paper bag bursting as he watched the dog's big tail crash in happiness against a rosebush and send up big clouds of driveway dust, in which a few petals swirled, then fluttered lazily to the ground.

YOUNG BOY: *May I interrupt?*

You may indeed. This is the end of a chapter, and, besides, you've been most attentive.

YOUNG BOY: *Well, I like the big dog and I'm sorry about the streetcar, but I'd like to hear about those robbers. There hasn't been a word about them.*

I was going to get to the robbers after the next chapter, which was to be concerned with Mrs. Montague's unfortunate tea party.

YOUNG BOY: *Can't we wait a bit for the tea party?*

I don't see why not. On, then, to the robbers.

YOUNG BOY: *And may I remind you that we haven't heard very much about the rabbit with the umbrella.*

I'd hoped you'd forgotten about him but I see you haven't. All right, all right; we'll get to him eventually.

William Pène du Bois

FOUR

Well, back on page twelve, in the prologue, you were quite right. The three robbers live in that haunted house down by the railroad tracks.

YOUNG BOY: *I told you so; that's just what I said.*

All right now; this is the beginning of a chapter and you mustn't interrupt.

Because they didn't have enough money to afford anything else, the three robbers lived in the haunted house. The window shutters banged late at night like gunshots, the stairs complained under unseen weights, and the death-watch beetles droned unsoothing songs. When the owls in nearby woods hooted, the three clutched one another in terror, for these robbers were not only hopelessly bad at their profession, they were timid men too.

Their names were Pease, Punch, and Mr. Bouncely.

Pease was the gunman of the gang, a tall, awkward man with large feet. He carried an enormous Webley-Vickers revolver in his coat pocket, so heavy that he was weighted down on one side and walked at a

63

slight list, like a ship heeling under a strong wind. He was frightened of the weapon, but Mr. Bouncely, the leader of the three, insisted that someone had to carry a gun. "No self-respecting gang would be without one," he said huffily, and he and Punch would take Pease out for revolver practice in empty fields far from human habitation. There, Punch and Mr. Bouncely behind him with their fingers in their ears, Pease would lift the enormous revolver in a trembling hand and point it at a tin can set on the ground in front of him. Invariably he missed and fired mile-long arching shots through the air. But Punch and Mr. Bouncely, whose eyes were tightly closed, applauded just as enthusiastically as if the shots had been accurate.

Then one night, much to Pease's relief, the gun was left out in the rain and all the parts rusted together; even after this Mr. Bouncely insisted it be taken along on their robbery attempts. "Regardless of its condition, no self-respecting gang should be without a gun—I mean a 'gat'—or is it a 'gut'?" asked Mr. Bouncely, who talked out of the corner of his mouth as good robbers do but often couldn't remember the proper words.

"It's 'gat,' " Punch instructed him.

Punch, the second of the three, was a man with a large stomach, which jiggled as he walked briskly on his way to buy burglar tools; and when he ran from watchdogs and policemen it bounced. He was fond of good food—in fact, food was always on his mind. The established practice when the three robbers entered a house to burgle it was that Punch would go straight to the kitchen to cook supper for himself, Pease, and Mr. Bouncely. If the refrigerator was well stocked Punch cooked up a sumptuous and tasty meal indeed, and their unknowing hosts would come home from a late motion-picture show to find a plate of chicken bones and a half-finished plum pudding on the kitchen table and a sink full of dishes to wash.

Often Punch's craving for food got the three of them into trouble. Once, when creeping through a large house in Schenectady-on-the-Vale, Mr. Bouncely bumped into Punch in the blackness and called out nervously, "Who's that?" Punch, munching on a pecan nut he'd found in a bowl in the hall, tried to reassure him that it was only Punch, but his mouth was full and instead he said, "Woompf!" At this Mr. Bouncely gave a terrible cry of terror and, after beating around the dark house like a frightened canary in a cage, he rushed out the front door and didn't return to their hideaway for a week. When he finally came back he explained to Punch and Pease that he'd bumped into the biggest watchdog in Schenectady-on-the-Vale, if not east of the Mississippi, and no amount of argument by Punch or Pease could persuade him otherwise. "It made a terrible gnashing sound," Mr. Bouncely said, and because he started to tremble thinking about it Punch and Pease gave up trying to convince him that it had been really only Punch.

Mr. Bouncely, though the leader of the group, was the most timid of them all. He was always hearing things late at night in other people's houses. Just as Punch would be putting a silver candlestick in a sack and Pease working on the lock of a safe, Mr. Bouncely would whisper hoarsely, "Hark!" After a minute of listening to the house creak around them, Mr. Bouncely would call out, "Who's that?" or, sometimes, "Help!

Help!" and the three of them, hearts in throats, frightened even more by their own shouts of terror, would drop everything and flee.

Many were the couples asleep in their upstairs bedrooms who, if not awakened by the slamming of the refrigerator door and the *whir-whir* of the egg-beater as Punch whipped up an omelet, were certainly jarred out of their sleep by hearing a voice cry out below, "Who's that? *Who's that?*" followed by terrible cries and the sounds of bodies bumping into furniture.

The house-owners would get up from their beds and, clutching their bathrobes tight around them, creep down the stairs to find a few burglary tools on the carpet—a screwdriver or a hammer perhaps. But none of their possessions would be missing, although the open front door swung softly to and fro in the night winds.

As you might suspect, Pease, Punch, and Mr. Bouncely were not particularly successful robbers. In fact, up to the time of their arrival in Adams they'd never managed to steal *anything*. They either frightened themselves out of their victims' houses by Mr. Bouncely's shouting, "Hark!" or "Who's that?" or "Run for your lives!" as we've seen, or Mr. Bouncely's master plans simply didn't work. Mr. Bouncely spent considerable time planning their operations—sometimes years of careful plotting with slide rules, hour glasses, barometers, and secret maps—but invariably difficulties arose that he hadn't counted on.

He had spent three weeks, for example, planning the burglary of a lighthouse some miles off the coast of Massachusetts, and was justifiably proud of his work. He had an accurate plan of the lighthouse; he knew where the cash box and a child's piggy-bank were; and he knew what time the lighthouse keeper and his family went to bed. Unfortunately, the night they picked to row out and burgle the lighthouse was an especially black one, and a foggy one as well, and although Mr. Bouncely was perched up in the bow with a slide rule, an hour glass, and some other pieces of equipment (including his roll of secret maps), they missed the lighthouse by a mile or so. They were picked up at dawn by a fishing boat, tired, but unflagging, Mr. Bouncely calling out the stroke to Pease and Punch at the oars as the little boat crept over the seas toward Ireland.

So when they reached Adams the three robbers were tired and penniless. Punch looked wasted and the stomach that was his pride had deflated to the flatness of an ironing board. Pease was so weak that the enormous, rusted Webley-Vickers revolver in his coat pocket made him sag to one side, like a ship listing in a hurricane.

Only Mr. Bouncely had a spark of enthusiasm left. The second day in Adams he called a meeting in the

William Péne du Bois

basement of the haunted house. The three robbers sat around a wooden table on which a candle set in a bottle flickered its thin flame. Finally Mr. Bouncely, his face as pale as a snowman's, drew a deep breath and then snarled out of the corner of his mouth, as all good gangsters should, "Very well, you gubs."

" 'Guys' is the word," Punch corrected. " 'Okay, you guys' is the way it should be said."

"Thank you, Punch," Mr. Bouncely said. "Okay, you guys," he continued, "here's the fitch."

"No, no," said Pease wearily. "It's 'pitch.' Here's the pitch."

"I shall never learn these gangster terms," Mr. Bouncely said gloomily. But he did his best, and under the helpful direction of Pease and Punch he managed to unfold his scheme—a plan to rob the largest house in Adams. This house stood near the top of Willow Hill, and was none other than Mr. Montague's house.

"A masterpiece," said Pease when Mr. Bouncely had finished.

"Does this house have a large and well-stocked kitchen?" asked Punch, whose empty stomach occasionally growled so angrily as to make Mr. Bouncely start in sudden fright.

"I believe so," replied Mr. Bouncely. "In fact," he whispered tensely as Punch and Pease leaned across the table with eyes wide in expectation, "I believe a turkey was delivered to the house yesterday."

The three sagged back in their seats and Punch said, "My, my." Not even a particularly unsoothing note by a death-watch beetle or a very nearby owl hooting sharply could startle them out of their comfortable thoughts of turkey and walnut stuffing and cold roast potatoes. They sat silent, their shadows thrown against the cellar walls by the guttering candle.

Finally Mr. Bouncely stirred in his seat and announced, "All right, boys; let's check our equipment."

Pease and Punch collected their burglary tools and stood waiting.

"Sack," Mr. Bouncely called, and Punch held up the huge burlap bag which had remained ever empty.

"Bimmy," he called out; and Pease corrected, "Jimmy," and produced the long wedge that robbers use to pry open windows.

"Gun"; and Pease brought out the Webley-Vickers revolver and waved it nervously.

"Secret maps"; and there was a hurried search, which disclosed them to be in Mr. Bouncely's hip pocket.

"Cooking utensils"; and the clatter of cutlery sounded as Punch patted his coat pocket.

"Flapjack"; and Punch replied, "We lost it two years ago. Besides, it's a 'blackjack,' not a 'flapjack.'"

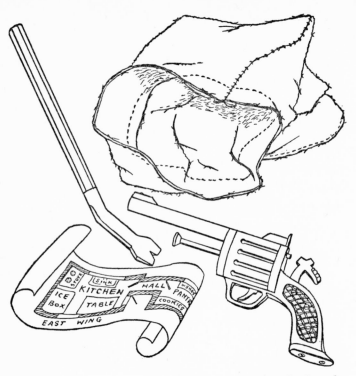

"I'd forgotten," said Mr. Bouncely. He looked at the other two. "Then we're ready," he whispered and puffed out the candle.

Up the cellar stairs and through the creaking house crept the three; then down the warped veranda steps into a moonlight that shone on the fields as soft as mist.

Almost immediately Mr. Bouncely's careful plans were put to the test. For as the three crossed the dark field, already crouched like Indians and *ssshushing* one another (though they were two miles at least from Mr. Montague's house), a curious and frightening thing happened. As they approached the thick hedge bordering the field they heard the purring of a car motor on the other side, then a gnashing of gears, and with a terrible roar the rear end of a car burst through the hedge with a great crackling of branches. It stopped, half in, half out of the hedge, its rear lights staring at the three startled robbers like the red eyes of a monster. A thin, ghostly voice floated from somewhere in the hedge. "Oh ye gods and little fishes," the voice announced. "I simply can't, can't, can't."

"Spooks!" shouted Mr. Bouncely, rooted to the ground.

A horn blew peevishly, and with a sudden lurch the car backed into the field and began to turn. Its front lights swept in a brilliant arc, lighting up in sharp outline scores of rabbits feeding on young corn shoots, and then the horrified forms of Pease, Punch, and Mr. Bouncely, throwing their huge shadows against the walls of the haunted house behind them.

"Run," shouted Mr. Bouncely. "Run for your lives!" Suiting action to words, he turned and moved off at enormous speed across the field to the woods, followed by Pease, Punch, and a group of frightened rabbits.

Behind them the faint, shrill barking of a dog suddenly sounded. "Bloodhounds!" Mr. Bouncely shouted and, increasing his speed, his arms and legs moving like locomotive pistons, he outdistanced Pease, Punch, and the rabbits and disappeared, with a crackling of branches, into the woods.

Pease, Punch, and one or two of the rabbits continued together, finally dropping, exhausted, into a ditch near the railroad tracks. Above them the moon shone full and bright, and Punch looked into Pease's pale face and asked, "What was it, Pease?"

"What was what?"

"What was it we ran away from?"

"Well, it looked like the rear end of a car," replied Pease. "But Mr. Bouncely said it was a spook, and Mr. Bouncely's word is good enough for me." He mopped his brow with a large handkerchief and shivered.

"I'm afraid we've lost Mr. Bouncely," said Punch, peeking over the edge of the ditch.

"So we've lost Mr. Bouncely," Pease agreed. "What are we going to do?"

"Well, I'm hungry," said Punch, watching a rabbit hop off to his corn shoots. "I keep thinking of that turkey."

"You mean you think we ought to go on, go on without Mr. Bouncely?" asked Pease breathlessly.

"Perhaps we ought to try calling him," suggested Punch, and the two rose to their feet and, cupping their hands to their mouths, shouted into the night, "*Mr. Bouncely! Mr. Bouncely!*" The call drifted across the darkened fields and through the forests. They called again and finally heard a distant shout—unfortunately, not one of response to their call but one of reheightened terror—then a faint crackling of branches as, presumably, Mr. Bouncely tore off even farther into the night.

"I'm afraid we've frightened him," said Pease. The two sat down again to think. Finally Punch's stomach gave a particularly angry growl and he said, "Look here, Pease, we've got to go on."

"Do you really think we ought to, Punch?" Pease asked. "I mean, traipse around at night through fields where the rear ends of cars hurtle at you through thick hedges? And without Mr. Bouncely?"

"We must take our chances," announced Punch solemnly.

So Pease and Punch crept out of the ditch and started the long walk up hill toward the Montague house. Occasionally they were frightened into ditches by the small sounds weasels and moles make in the forest at night, but finally they reached the head of the Montague driveway, squeaked open the gate, and entered the garden. The house was before them, the moon, huge above the roof, plumped down on a chimney like an overstuffed white cat. Pease clenched his enormous Webley-Vickers revolver, and, crossing the moon-soaked lawn, the two climbed into the house through an open window. Without a sound, Punch's sensitive nose finding the way, they moved through the warm dark house to the kitchen.

"We're here," breathed Punch. He opened the icebox door. The little light went on and showed a turkey

76

William Pène du Bois

so large and so perfectly cooked that Punch was quite beside himself. "It's a bird fit for a duke," he whispered hoarsely, his nervousness gone. Tenderly he drew the turkey forth and set it on the kitchen table. He and Pease hunched up two chairs behind them, they tucked napkins under their chins, and by the light of the moon flooding through the kitchen windows they attacked the bird with such a vengeance that only a few picked bones remained on the platter.

"Ah," said Punch, patting his stomach. "A superb

bird. I shall have to leave a note, complimenting the cook of the house."

"We've done a terrible thing," announced Pease.

"What's that?" asked Punch nervously.

"There's no turkey left," replied Pease. "There's none to take back to poor Mr. Bouncely. He'll be furious."

The two sat and thought. Then Pease said, "I have an idea, Punch."

"What?"

Pease looked about the kitchen, then whispered over the turkey bones, "We're robbers, aren't we?"

"We are," agreed Punch.

"Well, wouldn't Mr. Bouncely be pleased if perhaps we—we did a bit of—well, if we burgled a few things?"

Punch shivered. "Do you think we ought to?" he asked. "After all, these nice people have supplied us with a turkey."

"But we've got to bring Mr. Bouncely *something*," insisted Pease.

"I suppose you're right," agreed Punch. "All right, we'll burgle, but very small things, so small the owners of this house won't notice they've gone."

So Pease and Punch left the kitchen and crept through the house to find two very small objects to put in the large burlap bag. And they did. Pease found a pincushion with one pin stuck in it and Punch found a pawn from Mr. Montague's chess set. These they dropped into the bag, then climbed through the window and ran across the garden, sensing behind them the angry bulk of the white house and the disapproving stares of its many dark windows.

They ran gallumphing through the warm night to the haunted house, the burlap bag bouncing limply from Pease's shoulder. The noise the weasels and moles make in the forest went unheard in the flight of their heavy boots down the tar road. They ran across the cornfields, the rabbits fanning out in front of them, and paused only when they'd reached the veranda steps. "Oh, my," Punch panted. "What a jolting to give such a fine turkey dinner!" And he rubbed his stomach gingerly.

"Do you suppose Mr. Bouncely has come back?" Pease asked, peering into the dark doorway.

"Let's shout for him," suggested Punch. He and Pease cupped their hands to their mouths and shouted, *"Mr. Bouncely! Mr. Bouncely!"* They heard the sudden scamper of feet and the slam of a door upstairs inside the house. "That must be him," said Pease. The two entered the house, lit a candle, and went upstairs to see.

79

They finally discovered him crouched in a clothes closet. "Oh, it's you," said Mr. Bouncely, his face pale in the candlelight.

"What are you doing in there?" asked Punch.

"Resting," replied Mr. Bouncely quickly. "Resting from a nightmare of an experience in the woods."

"We've been burgling," exclaimed Pease excitedly. "We burgled the white house on the hill."

Mr. Bouncely stared at them. "Why didn't you wait for me?" he asked. "No self-respecting gang goes about burgling without its leader."

"We called for you," explained Punch. "We shouted from a railroad ditch."

"Well, I heard nothing," Mr. Bouncely said. "Except"—and his face paled at the thought of it—"the barking of bloodhounds and one or two owls calling out my name." He paused. "But no matter," he continued more brightly. "Did you bring back some food?"

"We forgot," Punch said simply.

Mr. Bouncely moaned as he shuffled out of the clothes closet. He led the way to the cellar, where the table was cleared and the candle set in a bottle.

"Well," said Mr. Bouncely wearily, "let's see the boot."

" 'Loot' is the word, Mr. Bouncely. 'Loot,' " said

Pease gently, for he didn't want to hurt Mr. Bouncely's
feelings. He took the burlap bag by the corners at the
bottom and shook it. Nothing happened. He shook it
hard until, at last, out rolled the pawn and the pincushion.

Mr. Bouncely leaned over the table and peered at
these objects for a long time. Then he picked up the
pawn. "What's this?" he asked.

"I believe it's a pawn. A white pawn from a chess
set," explained Punch.

"I don't suppose it's edible," said Mr. Bouncely sadly, testing it with his teeth to make sure. "And this," he continued, picking up the pincushion, "I suppose, is a pincushion."

"With one pin in it," said Pease.

Mr. Bouncely put the pincushion and the pawn on the table and looked at them. "Well," he said, "I'm not sure our first robbery has been too successful." But then, seeing the crestfallen faces of Pease and Punch, he added hastily, "Not that you haven't done a fine job. But," he continued, "these objects seem to me rather on the small side."

"Small!" echoed Pease and Punch.

"They're too small," repeated Mr. Bouncely. "If we're to be successful we must burgle *huge* things." And he made an expansive sweep of his arms that knocked over the candle, plunging the cellar room into darkness. "Who's there?" shouted Mr. Bouncely, frightened. "What's happened?" He jumped from his chair, prepared to run up the cellar stairs. He was quieted down by Punch while Pease relit the candle.

"Well, what do you think we ought to do?" asked Punch when Mr. Bouncely was calm enough to continue.

"We must burgle *huge* things," Mr. Bouncely repeated.

THE RABBIT'S UMBRELLA

"But where?" asked Pease and Punch.

Mr. Bouncely bowed his head in thought, then looked up. "Were there large objects in the house you were in this evening?" he asked.

"Yes, there were," replied Pease and Punch. "There were very large things, such as oaken chests, a grand piano we saw in the shadows, a grandfather clock—"

"Was there, for example," Mr. Bouncely asked slowly, "a large turkey?"

"We ate it," Pease replied shamefacedly.

Mr. Bouncely moaned again. "But was it a large kitchen where one might find food besides the turkey—such as a can of peas, maybe, or a crust or two of bread?"

"Oh, certainly," replied Punch. "It was a large kitchen indeed."

Mr. Bouncely breathed deeply. "That decides it," he said. "We'll get a good night's rest and tomorrow we'll go back and burgle the same house."

"A masterpiece of a plan," declared Pease and Punch. "They'll never expect to be burgled twice in two nights." They clasped their hands in admiration and looked at Mr. Bouncely.

YOUNG BOY: *If this is the end of the chapter, may I ask some questions?*

You may. Go right ahead.

YOUNG BOY: *When Mr. Bouncely was wandering around in the forest did he see the rabbit with the umbrella?*

No. It was too dark.

YOUNG BOY: *Is there really a rabbit with an umbrella in the woods?*

Certainly. Probably flocks of them, but it was dark and Mr. Bouncely couldn't see them.

YOUNG BOY: *Did the one or two owls really call out his name?*

No. The owls couldn't have called out his name, Mr. Bouncely being new in the neighborhood, and they not knowing who he was. What he heard, of course, were the voices of Pease and Punch, shouting in the distance.

YOUNG BOY: *And what was that car doing, bursting through hedges and backing about the field?*

That is explained in the next chapter which—if you'll allow me to proceed—has to do with Mrs. Montague's unfortunate tea party.

FIVE

Mrs. Montague's tea party, as you might suspect, was not a success but just another setback in a day full of unpleasantness. First, just as Mrs. Montague had started clipping and snipping among her flowers, the cook entered the living room and announced, "Ma'am, the turkey's clean gone."

"What?" asked Mrs. Montague.

"The turkey's clean gone."

"Clean gone?"

"Well, ma'am, the plate's there, and there're some bones on the plate, but what most folks imagine as turkey is clean gone."

Mrs. Montague went out to the kitchen and, sure enough, a finger poked at the platter produced only the dry clink of picked bones. "Dear me," said Mrs. Montague—for the turkey was to have been used for tea-party sandwiches. She and the cook decided finally that the cinnamon toast, the thinly sliced cucumber sandwiches, the pumpkin seeds in bowls, and the sponge cake, would have to do. Mrs. Montague left the kitchen, feeling that her day was not going well.

85

THE RABBIT'S UMBRELLA

As she walked through the hall she heard the commotion out on the driveway—the scraping of something against the driveway gravel and the heavy breathing of men at work. She guessed that her new poodle, Minnehaha, was arriving in a large box. She called eagerly to Peter, who was driving about the house in his little car with the three carts attached behind. The two of them went to the front door and looked out into the front garden.

"Minnehaha," whispered Mrs. Montague. She hoped Mr. Perkins had trained the poodle to do tricks —such as playing dead, rolling over, sitting up on his haunches, or shaking hands (either with his left paw or his right; it didn't make the slightest difference as long as her guests at tea parties said, "Oh, how charming Minnehaha is, how divine Minnehaha is!")

Peter was jumping up and down like a bobbin on a string. He had a tadpole in a glass of water he wanted to show the dog, and there were some fine places in the back garden he'd discovered that morning that wanted digging into and investigation by a boy's shovel and a dog's dusky nose.

Mrs. Montague was appalled when the big dog crowded through the garden gate. Her first thought was that a large man was standing beside her husband, bundled to the ears in a fur coat; someone, perhaps,

Mr. Montague had met downtown and had asked for lunch. When she realized that the creature was a dog her hands fluttered nervously to her throat and she called out just what she did a few chapters ago, "Oh, Henry. That's *not* a poodle. How could you?"

THE RABBIT'S UMBRELLA

Her dislike of dogs returned instantly, her old fears of muddy paw marks, bones, and tufts of hair cluttering her house increased tenfold. For surely this dog would leave paw marks the size of dinosaur tracks; the gnawed thighbones of elephants would rattle under her feet; she'd discover tufts of dog hair like bundles of hay scattered throughout the house. When the enormous dog came in the front door and padded heavily down the hall to the living room, she felt that her home had diminished to the size of a doll's house. She faced her husband and stamped her foot angrily. "Henry," she said. "You must take that creature back immediately."

"Not on your life," answered Mr. Montague, sitting down heavily in his armchair and patting his brow with a large white handkerchief.

"Oh, Mother," cried Peter, hanging on the dog's neck. "Don't send him back. He's big and wonderful and his name is Lump." He nuzzled Lump's ear, and in appreciation the dog's tail swept like an oar across the room, collecting a glass vase on the way and smashing it to bits on the floor.

"Oh!" shouted Mrs. Montague. "*Look* what the creature's done."

"He didn't mean to, Mother."

"That is hardly an excuse," replied his mother firmly. "Now, Peter, climb down from the dog's neck and go to your room. I want to talk to your father alone."

Peter hesitated but, seeing the look in his mother's eyes, he climbed down from Lump's neck and shuffled obediently from the room. The dog's tail stopped moving and he froze in a curiously stiff attitude of dejection.

THE RABBIT'S UMBRELLA

Mrs. Montague cleared her throat. "Henry, what are we going to do?"

"I don't know," said Mr. Montague wearily.

"What are we going to feed him? Why, he'd finish off an ox a day. Think of the bills."

"I know," replied Mr. Montague.

"I think you'd better take him right back to Mr. Perkins' pet shop."

"I simply haven't the strength, Harriet," Mr. Montague admitted. "I have blisters on my feet; my back aches; my knees are wobbly. I feel as though I'd moved a trunk of books in here, not a dog."

"Well, then," said Mrs. Montague, "I suppose we'll have to wait till Monday. But then he really must be taken back and exchanged for a smaller, a more reasonable dog. Don't you agree, Henry?"

"I suppose so," said Mr. Montague. "He'll have to go. Though it's too bad; Peter seems so attached to him." He looked at his wife. "Perhaps you'll change your mind over the week-end."

"Not a chance," replied Mrs. Montague. "For the life of me, Henry, I can't see what induced you to buy him. Look at him."

Mr. Montague inspected the dog. He had to admit that he found little similarity between the dog his son affectionately called Lump and the sleek, eager, long-tailed dog that stalked the bronze deer in the clubhouse library. It was quite obvious that he had somehow made a bad mistake. "I'll take him back Monday," he announced.

Peter was furious when his parents told him that Lump was to be returned. He locked himself in his room and said he wasn't going to talk to anyone, not even the cook, for a whole year. And as for eating—he wasn't going to eat for *two* years.

So you can see what a miserable Saturday it had started out to be, not only for Mrs. Montague but for everybody. Mr. Montague's back hurt; his wife hadn't a poodle for her tea party; his son Peter was not only to lose his new pet but had promised himself neither to talk nor eat for a year or so, and *that* was going to be most trying. Lump felt unwanted and lay dejectedly in the living-room corner, without so much as a spark of interest in a beetle that crossed in front of his nose, going from somewhere to somewhere with a bread crumb in its pincers.

The tea party itself didn't do much to improve Mrs. Montague's day, though the sun was shining and the tea urn and cooky plates on the tables set out on the terrace glittered prettily.

Dr. Trimble was the first to arrive. He came early to parties, for, old and short-sighted, he liked to find a comfortable seat where he could eat thinly sliced cucumber sandwiches and talk about his travels across the world and the curious things he had seen. Few people believed a word he said. On his way through the living room to the terrace with Mrs. Montague he noticed Lump, sitting silent and dejected by the sofa. "Great Heavens," he exclaimed. "What's *that?*" He stopped and peered through his thick-rimmed spectacles.

"He's just staying for the week-end," Mrs. Montague explained, wishing she'd shut the dog up in the kitchen.

"A friend of your husband?" asked Dr. Trimble. "Surely not."

"It's a dog," announced Mrs. Montague simply.

"Surely not," said Dr. Trimble again. He inspected the dog closely and prodded it with the tip of his cane. "It's stuffed," he said. "It's stuffed, and what's more it's a stuffed panda. How very nice for your husband to have had the chance to collect such a fine specimen on his trip through the Himalayas!"

"My husband has never been to the Himalayas," Mrs. Montague said.

"Stuff and nonsense," said Dr. Trimble. "Of course he's been to the Himalayas. How else could he collect a panda bear, and such a fine specimen too?" He turned toward the terrace, where Mrs. Montague placed him next to a table of sandwiches and poured him a cup of tea. She left to go indoors and see that Lump was sent to the kitchen, but guests started to arrive and, involved in her duties as hostess, she soon forgot him.

Out on the terrace Dr. Trimble consumed cucumber sandwiches and nodded silently at the guests as they spread out across the terrace, among the tea tables, and on the lawn. "Mr. Mirabelle!" he called suddenly and pounded his cane on the paving stones. A young man detached himself from his friends and approached.

"You on the mayor's council?" asked Dr. Trimble.

"I certainly am," said young Mr. Mirabelle proudly, and he sat down opposite Dr. Trimble and arranged one leg carefully over the other, hoisting the crease along his trouser leg slightly. He leaned forward intently. "I certainly am, Doctor Trimble," he repeated.

"Well, you're a bunch of lily-footed nincompoops!" exclaimed Dr. Trimble.

"I beg your pardon," said Mr. Mirabelle.

"I said you're a bunch of lily-footed nincompoops," repeated Dr. Trimble. "You have no more right to run this town than a bunch of fieldmice."

"But why?" asked Mr. Mirabelle, fidgeting in his chair.

"The streetcar, of course. You've taken away our streetcar."

"But it was old, Doctor Trimble, and getting in the way."

Dr. Trimble snorted. "May I remind you," he said, "that respected people in this community are very wary about throwing old things away. Look in the home of the decent citizen and you'll see plenty of things that are old and get in the way—hound dogs as old as God, for instance; women's hats bought in the last century; buffalo robes the Indians must have used; fur coats with the arms eaten off by moths; grandfather clocks with pendulums missing; old books with paper as stiff and yellow as parchment; chairs so weak with age no one's allowed to sit in them. And what about all the wonderful things that are stored in attics?—tennis balls with no bounce left, skates that don't fit, roller-skate keys, paintings of great-aunts, and trunks of old clothes. And in tool sheds—shuttlecocks with the feathers gone, croquet balls chewed by Irish setters, one oar, and old license plates. And you mean to tell me, young man, that you'd throw away any of these things without the most careful consideration, without taking whatever it is and turning it slowly in your hand and looking at it and thinking what it once meant to you and the days it recalls? Though it's old and in the way, don't you find yourself putting it back where you found it, feeling much better about the world as you do so, knowing you've saved something of value and something that will give you the pleasure of fine memories when you run across it again?

"Why do you suppose Mr. and Mrs. Montague clutter up their living room with that moth-eaten panda bear with the stuffing falling out of it? Because that thing in there brings back the wild Himalayas to Mr. Montague every time he walks through his living room, and that's mighty important to a man."

"But, Doctor Trimble, a streetcar is something quite different," Mr. Mirabelle started to say.

"Stuff and nonsense," said Dr. Trimble. "Mayors' councils," he continued, "should be composed of very old men who know the worth of the past, or very small boys who are living the best life—riding in streetcars, fishing for catfish, and walking in the cream-dust of summer roads—and will want to remember it."

"But Doctor Trimble—"

"Oh, dear me," said Mrs. Montague, overhearing the two, and if she hadn't been holding a tray of tomato sandwiches she would have wrung her hands.

"And what's to save us," Dr. Trimble was saying, "from mayors' councils that yank away our streetcars and are as likely as not to start in on our tool sheds, our garages, and our attics? Why, it's a serious matter, serious enough for the rabbit with the umbrella."

"What!" exclaimed Mr. Mirabelle.

"Oh, dear, *dear* me," said Mrs. Montague.

But at that moment there was a commotion in the living room. A sharp *yip-yip-yipping* pierced the pleasant, tea-tinkling conversation, a rush of heavy feet sounded, and Lump appeared at the terrace door, his eyes hugely round and staring. He paused only a second; then the *yip-yip* sounded behind him and he bolted through the party with his tail tucked tight between his legs, vaulted the hedge bordering the rose garden, and disappeared from view. A tea table brushed by his flight turned crazily on its round base and finally collapsed its load of cinnamon toast and anchovy sandwiches on the lawn.

"It's not stuffed," cried Dr. Trimble from his chair, his argument with Mr. Mirabelle forgotten. "Why, it's not stuffed at all, but on the contrary is a panda bear of exceptional vitality and speed."

"Ye gods and little fishes!" Heads turned to see, appearing through the terrace door, first a prancing miniature poodle, daintily stepping on his delicate paws, then a long red leash, and finally, at the end of the leash, Mrs. Phipps.

YOUNG BOY: *Is that the end of the tea-party chapter? Are we going on to the robbers and perhaps the rabbit with the umbrella?*

No indeed. This is the *middle* of a chapter, and middles of chapters mustn't be broken into. Quiet, please.

YOUNG BOY: *What a curious man Doctor Trimble is.*

Isn't he, though? Probably well worth listening to, but I assure you he'd turn silent as a fish if constantly interrupted, especially in the middle of a chapter.

You'll remember that Mrs. Phipps had just appeared at the terrace door, preceded by her poodle, Rasputin. Reaching out a limp gloved hand, Mrs. Phipps called shrilly, "My dear, dear Harriet," and advanced toward Mrs. Montague. "How wonderful to see you! My precious Rasputin has scared the most extraordinary *thing* out of your living room. What on earth, Harriet, was it?"

Mrs. Montague started to reply, but Mrs. Phipps

continued. "You know, my Rasputin is really the bravest creature in all the world." She looked fondly at Rasputin, who was inspecting the cinnamon toast and anchovies on the lawn and deciding that he preferred the cinnamon, which tickled his nose. "Let me tell you the most extraordinary thing that happened to me and Rasputin last night," said Mrs. Phipps, settling herself into a chair and accepting a cup of tea. The guests drew closer, and Mrs. Phipps munched quickly on a jam sandwich, then began.

"As you know," she said, "I have difficulty in putting my Ford in reverse. I can go forward, turn, and stop, and do all those sorts of things with no trouble whatsoever. But when it comes to backing up I seem all thumbs. I can't find the gearshift, I stall the car, and very often I simply have to get out and leave it where it is.

"Well, last night, coming home from a dinner party ten miles down the line in Dover, with Rasputin sitting up with me in the front seat, I thought I might get on a secluded lane where no one like Officer Delaney would be shouting at me and confusing me, and *practice* getting the Ford into reverse. So I did. On the way back I found a nice straight stretch of road that runs parallel to the meadow, with that old crumbling house standing in the middle. And there, with the moon shining and no one to see, I put the car into reverse. It was a most enjoyable experience. I backed the car for a mile or so, looking in the rear-view mirror sometimes, often over my shoulder, and even out the window, as I've seen truck drivers do. It was a most thrilling experience for one who has been so rarely in reverse."

Mrs. Phipps paused, rapidly consumed another jam sandwich, and, dropping a large piece of Mrs. Montague's expensive sponge cake into Rasputin's small jaws, continued. "But when it came time for me to go forward I discovered I simply couldn't. I wrestled with the gear, turned off the motor and started it again, and tried things of that sort, but the car would not go forward. It kept backing up until I thought, Oh my Heavens, I'll be back in Dover before I can say fiddlesticks. So in a terrible fit of anger, having absolutely no wish to go back to Dover, I mashed the accelerator to the floor. The car bounced backward in a great leap, turned, and piled into the large hedge bordering the field.

"As I sat there in the hedge with a large branch that had brushed through the window, suddenly the solution came to me. Said I to myself, 'I'll back the car into the meadow, turn it around, back it through the hedge again (but this time face its rear end toward Adams), and back up the car the two miles to my home.' Even driving backward it shouldn't have been too difficult, and indeed it wasn't.

"But as I turned the car in the meadow I saw a most curious and terrifying spectacle. I'd blown my horn carefully, then backed the car out of the hedge. As I turned, the headlights swept across the field and lighted up, to my astonishment, the forms of three men—or what I thought were men. They may have been—well, ghosts." Mrs. Phipps shivered and rapidly consumed yet another jam sandwich.

"It was Rasputin, my darling Rasputin, who drove them away," she continued. "He merely curled his lip and barked, and the three creatures turned on their heels and disappeared across the field at extraordinary speed."

"But what were these creatures?" asked an elderly woman, peering in awe at Rasputin through her pince-nez.

Dr. Trimble stirred in his chair. "It is my considered opinion," he said, "that the three men were Chinese tea merchants." The group turned toward him in surprise, but no further information was forthcoming; Dr. Trimble reached for a cucumber sandwich and settled back in his chair, silent.

"Well, I don't know," said Mrs. Phipps, off her stride. "I don't know who or what they were."

THE RABBIT'S UMBRELLA

Mrs. Montague was secretly pleased at Mrs. Phipps's discomfiture. She loathed Rasputin almost as much as she loathed Lump. Every time his name was mentioned or guests bent to coo and pat his head or a piece of her best sponge cake was dropped into his jaws, Mrs. Montague's hand shook and stains of tea spread across her Venetian tablecloth.

Lump, in the meantime, was snuffling along the bottom of the hedge, keeping a big eye out for the black animal which had jumped him from the living room.

From his window, Peter, who had been sulking in his room throughout the tea party, saw the dog and quickly ran down the back stairs through the kitchen to the vegetable garden. At his soft whistle, the big dog came padding joyfully around the hedge. "Lump," Peter whispered happily in his ear, and he led the dog through the kitchen and up the stairs to his room. There the two played—not roughhousing, but easily and quietly—as if they were old friends, Peter riding on Lump's back, swinging on the sweep of his tail like a trapeze artist. Sometimes he just ran his hands through the thick fur behind the dog's ears.

When the cook came to his room to tell him his supper was ready, Peter, very hungry indeed, decided he'd eat as long as Lump was in the house. When Lump was actually taken away—well, *then* he'd lock himself in his room and refuse to eat or speak to anyone for a year or so. So he and Lump went down to supper in the kitchen.

Outside on the lawn they could hear the tea party ending. A few people remained, their voices drifting across the lawn through the kitchen window. Once Lump's ears pricked at the sound of a high-pitched *yip*. And later they heard Dr. Trimble calmly saying, "I see no explanation necessary. It is quite evident that the three were Chinese tea merchants." Peter liked Dr. Trimble. They often talked together about pixies, dragons, rabbits with umbrellas, and the ponds where the mice skated in winter. Peter felt sure that Dr. Trimble would like Lump.

After supper the boy and the dog went back upstairs. When Mrs. Montague came up after her dinner with Mr. Montague she found Peter asleep, and Lump draped across the bottom of the bed, watching her with big, sad eyes. She tucked her son in and took the dog down to the living room. He padded along obediently behind her.

"You can sleep in here tonight," she said. "Monday, back you go." She watched him settle down at the foot of the sofa. She felt a twinge of shame at being so rude to the dog. But he *was* so large and unmanageable and, besides, he had disgraced her terribly by running from Mrs. Phipps's poodle.

"You wouldn't think a dog that size could be such a coward, would you?" she asked her husband as they prepared for bed. Mr. Montague grunted. His back still hurt. "It's been a hard day," he admitted as he eased himself into bed, "for everybody—including poor Lump."

Outside, a big moon shone down on Adams. Only the streetcar moved on its streets; Officer Delaney, Mr. Otway, and Dr. Trimble had decided to take it on a long spin through the night and talk of the good old days together. The rest of the town slept—except down in the haunted house, where Pease, Punch, and Mr. Bouncely prepared for the night's burglary.

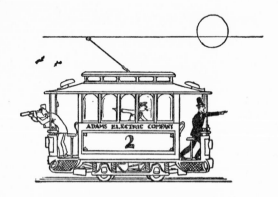

SIX

Through the cobwebbed basement windows the moon shone a sickly light into the robbers' council room. Mr. Bouncely, sitting at the head of the table, held his watch to the candle and peered at the time. "It's two o'clock," he announced. "I'm too hungry to stay in this place a moment longer. Besides, by now the roads should be clear. The bops will be in bed."

"A policeman is better referred to as a 'cop,' not a 'bop,'" corrected Punch. "He can also be called a 'flick,' a 'dick,' a 'bobby,' and, I believe, a 'gumshoe,' but never a 'bop.'"

"Very well," said Mr. Bouncely sadly. "The cops will be off the streets by now. It's time we set out." He stood up. "Now remember what I told you. After we've been to the kitchen and had supper we must remember to remove *huge* objects—not pawns and pincushions but the biggest objects we can lay our hands on."

As Punch and Pease nodded agreement Mr. Bouncely snuffed out the candle, and the three climbed the cellar steps and crept through the creaking house onto the veranda.

"I don't think we ought to cross that," said Mr. Bouncely nervously, pointing to the cornfield. "I'd rather we went around the long way."

Pease and Punch raised no objections. They had no wish to go near the hedge through which the rear ends of motorcars appeared with alarming swiftness. So they circled the field and set out up the country lanes warm with the night smells of honeysuckle. Once the streetcar rumbled past, its windows casting big moving squares of light against the forests and fields. The three robbers climbed out of the ditch where they had flung themselves and waited until the rattle of the streetcar had died in the distance; then they continued on their way.

They tiptoed up Willow Street. Near the Montague driveway Mr. Bouncely bolted at a scampering sound in the forest and had to be forcibly restrained from fleeing back to their hideaway. "It's those owls," he muttered, looking nervously into the trees. A bank of clouds sullenly crossed the moon, and the long weeping leaves of the willows stretched down to brush the robbers' faces like ghostly fingers. "Heavens!" said Punch, Pease, and especially Mr. Bouncely.

Finally they reached the driveway and their feet started to go *crunch-crunch-crunch* in the gravel. Mr. Bouncely stopped. He was unnerved by the crunching sound. "We're making too much noise," he said. "Three pairs of boots in the gravel sound like an express train. We'll wake someone up."

"Shall only one of us go?" asked Pease and Punch, looking at each other, then up the hill, where the dark bulk of the Montague house loomed.

"I have a better idea," said Mr. Bouncely. He turned to Punch. "If you carry Pease and me on your shoulders," he explained, "it will sound, if anyone happens to hear, like *one* person going up the driveway, not three."

Punch moaned loudly.

"Not so loud," whispered Mr. Bouncely, hopping up and down in consternation at the echoing strength of Punch's sorrowful cry.

Finally Punch was persuaded. He knelt down. Mr. Bouncely clambered on his back, then Pease clambered onto Mr. Bouncely's shoulders, and with a grunt Punch straightened up. The tall, teetering totem pole of robbers tottered up the driveway toward the front gate. But like all Mr. Bouncely's plans this one was not a success. For unless you've practiced carrying men on your back, as you might if you were a tumbler in a circus, you'd discover that balancing such a mighty weight as Mr. Bouncely and Pease and Pease's enormous Webley-Vickers revolver was a difficult task.

William Pène du Bois

Punch had never been a tumbler in a circus and to keep the other two upright he found himself tearing up and down the driveway like a boy balancing a long broomstick on the end of one finger.

They made considerable noise. Pease, at the top, as high as a small tree, kept up a constant nervous moan; Mr. Bouncely alternated calls of direction with pleas for silence ("Quiet. *Quiet!* QUIET!!"); and, at the bottom, Punch, his boots thrashing through the gravel, the kitchen cutlery clattering in his pocket, panted and groaned, "Steady up there, *steady*."

At the noise the forest woke up. The chipmunks and squirrels peered out from behind their stone walls and the crows took their heads from under the black blankets of their wings and watched in astonishment as Pease's head moved through the lower branches of their roosting trees. Up in the house on the hill Mr. Montague turned restlessly in his bed.

Finally Punch managed with terrible effort to reach the front gate; there Pease and Mr. Bouncely climbed down and the three collapsed, their backs against the gate, to recover their wind. "Well, we're here," whispered Mr. Bouncely, "and nothing seems to be stirring." Surprisingly, it was true. From behind them the moon shone on quiet fields and the Montague house sat in its shadows as still as a waiting cat. "Come on," said Mr. Bouncely, and he squeaked open the front gate.

"I think there's a window by the front door," Pease whispered in Mr. Bouncely's ear.

"Lead on, then," ordered Mr. Bouncely. "I'll be right behind you."

They skirted the dark shape of Peter's push-pedal car, standing on the garden path with the three carts attached to it, and reached the window. Pease opened the window with his jimmy and the three climbed into the warm darkness of the house. They stood in the hall, breathing heavily—especially Punch, who was still out of breath from his strenuous climb. "I'd like a glass of water," he said, leaning weakly against the window sill. "You can get some in the kitchen," replied Mr. Bouncely, "if you'll show us the way."

Guided by his sensitive nose, Punch led the way through the dining room and the pantry to the kitchen. "I smell cucumbers," he whispered over his shoulder. "And strawberry jam, cinnamon toast, the remains of a sponge cake, and pumpkin seeds in bowls."

Pease produced a candle from his pocket and lit it. Sure enough, the remains of the tea-party sandwiches lay spread before them on the kitchen table. While Pease and Mr. Bouncely started in on the sandwiches Punch mixed a fruit salad. They had coffee to finish off the meal. Mr. Bouncely commented he'd had so many sandwiches he felt he'd been on a five-day picnic, but he seemed considerably cheered. He leaned back in his kitchen chair and patted his stomach. "Aaaaah," he said expansively.

"Are we going to burgle now?" asked Pease.

Mr. Bouncely's chair came down on the floor with a bang. His face fell. "Mercy," he whispered nervously. "I suppose we ought to."

Pease swallowed hard and had another glass of water.

"Yes, we must," Mr. Bouncely went on regretfully. "After all, it's our profession." He looked at them. "I'm afraid there's no point in discussing it. Are we ready?"

Pease and Punch nodded. Mr. Bouncely blew out the candle, the kitchen was plunged in darkness, and the three men set out through the house.

The living room was shrouded in deep shadows; it was so quiet that it seemed as if a sudden noise *must* break the silence—a window shade snapping up suddenly, the grand piano folding its three legs and collapsing in a heap of twanging wires and flailing hammers, the grandfather clock crashing to the floor like a dead man from a closet—*something*. But the three men heard only the beating of their hearts in the darkness. "Is this where you found the pawn and the pincushion?" whispered Mr. Bouncely.

"Yes," was the reply.

"Let's search around for something a bit larger," ordered Mr. Bouncely.

Pease made the first discovery. "There's a big chest over here by the fireplace," he announced softly.

Mr. Bouncely crept across the room, his toes curling in excitement. He was convinced that all chests were full of doubloons and rotting Spanish veils. "Can you lift it?" he asked.

"It's very heavy," admitted Pease. "I can't budge it."

Mr. Bouncely opened the lid and felt inside. "It feels like firewood," he said. He scratched his head solemnly.

"Hist!" called Punch excitedly from across the room. "There's something down here on the floor by the sofa. It feels like a sack."

"A sack?" asked Mr. Bouncely. "Is it full?"

"It's bulging full," replied Punch. "And it's big, awful big."

"Excellent," breathed Mr. Bouncely; he felt almost as happy about sacks as he did about chests. "Let's pick it up and clear out. We'll open it down in the hideaway. I fancy it will be full of silver candlesticks and, well—all sorts of things." He and Pease crept through the darkness to Punch's side. "Can you lift it?" asked Mr. Bouncely. "Barely," Punch grunted. "Give him a hand, Pease," whispered Mr. Bouncely.

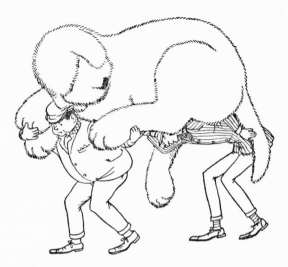

Pease bent in the darkness, and with a whispered *heave-ho* he and Punch lifted the slumbering Lump into the air. Lump was snoring, but so gently that neither Pease, Punch, nor Mr. Bouncely heard him.

"Quickly, quickly!" said Mr. Bouncely tensely. "Follow me." He led them to the hall. Oh, my, he thought. At last—a successful burglary! But as he paused to search for the handle to the front door he heard a deep, rhythmic breathing behind him. "Hark!" he whispered loudly. He listened. There it was again, not the quick, nervous panting of Pease and Punch, but a low rumble that sounded like a freight train in the distance. "Who's there?" he called out. There was no answer. "Do you hear anything, Pease? Punch?"

"Yes," squeaked Punch. "There's someone here in the hall. I can hear him breathing."

"*Run!*" shouted Mr. Bouncely. "*Run for your lives!*" He tore open the front door and rushed into the garden.

There in the moonlight he saw Peter's car with the three carts attached behind, standing on the garden path. "Quick," he called. "Bundle the sack in the first cart and get yourselves into the others. We'll make a quick getaway. Hurry!" He squeezed himself behind the little steering wheel of Peter's car with difficulty. Pease and Punch dropped Lump into the first cart, Punch climbed into the second, which complained with a shrill squeal of axles under his weight, and Pease clambered into the third cart, where he sat with his long bony legs drawn up in front of him.

A light went on in the second story of the house. "They're coming after us," shouted Pease, looking up from the back cart. "Hurry, hurry!"

"I can't find the starter," replied Mr. Bouncely, searching frantically on the tiny dashboard. "I can't get the car started."

"Maybe the starter and the accelerator are on the same pedal," suggested Punch from the second cart.

"Possibly," replied Mr. Bouncely. He searched with his feet and discovered the truth. "Oh, mercy!" he

114

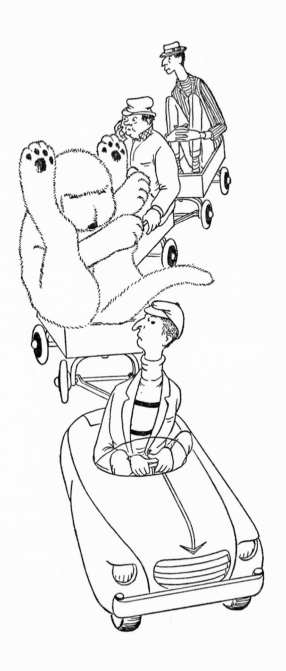

yelled. "This isn't a real car; it's a push-pedal car." He made an effort to get out but was stuck in the cramped space as solidly as a cork in a champagne bottle.

"Push-pedal it, then," shouted Punch behind him. "But hurry, hurry!"

There wasn't much else to be done so Mr. Bouncely applied his feet to the pedals and pushed manfully, pulling back from the tiny steering wheel and driving hard with his legs. The car and its three carts inched toward the garden gate.

"Faster," yelled Punch. "You're barely moving us."

The sweat was pouring off Mr. Bouncely's forehead. He clenched his teeth, he gripped the tiny steering wheel, and he strained against the pedals. Finally they moved through the gate and as Mr. Bouncely turned down the driveway the car began to gather momentum, coasting at increasing speed, with the carts rattling along behind. The wind began to sweep against their faces. The gravel flew out from beneath the tin wheels with a sharp crackle.

"Don't overdo it," yelled Punch. "Not too fast."

"There are no brakes," replied Mr. Bouncely over his shoulder. "There's no horn, there's no gasoline gauge, there's no speedometer, there's no nothing." His legs moved up and down vigorously on the whirling pedals. "There's nothing to be done, nothing."

THE RABBIT'S UMBRELLA

His cart went over a stone with a sharp bump, and Lump, lying motionless in the second cart, woke up.

Lump had had perhaps the most trying day of anybody in this book. He had been heaved and hauled through Mr. Perkins' pet shop; hoisted through Officer Delaney's traffic jam; shoved like a packing case up a gravel driveway into a house where he wasn't appreciated and out of which he was chased by a sharp-toed poodle. That night he had gone to sleep by the living-room sofa hoping that the next day would show a turn for the better, that he would awaken to find affection, a bowlful of dog biscuits, and a back yard cluttered with old bones. He didn't expect to wake up in a bouncing cart, to look up to see black trees whirring by against a moon, or to hear the roar of tin tires, rushing through the gravel. And when he struggled to a sitting position Lump didn't expect to look ahead to see a man hunched over in a midget automobile; or to look back over his shoulder to see the terrified face, white in the bright moonlight, of a man as big and round as a beachball; or still farther back, in another cart, a man as tall as a telephone pole. It was all too much for Lump, as it might be for anybody. Deep in his stomach there gathered and rolled up his throat and out along his tongue into the night a wild, drawn-out cry of fright and misery and dejection and anger; and this cry rolled across the meadows and the forests like a thunderclap.

The cry awakened the countryside. The turtle in the country club swimming pool, asleep under his green, chlorinated blanket, heard nothing, but others did. The chipmunks and the squirrels peered out from behind stone walls, and the crows scratched angrily on their pine-tree perches and decided that Adams County was no place for a good night's rest. In the town of Adams a few lights were switched on and people looked from their windows; in Harry's Diner forks clattered to the counter and heads turned to the screen door, as if expecting that whatever had made the noise might walk in, filling the doorway with its dark body; in Mrs. Phipps's bedroom Rasputin heard it, and he crept under a footstool and began to whimper. Mr. Montague, who had seen Peter's car and cart disappearing through the gate, heard it, Lump's long cry, as he ran through his garden in his bedroom slippers and bathrobe.

And, of course, Pease, Punch, and Mr. Bouncely heard it.

"Hey!" shouted Punch.

"Is that a police siren?" yelled Mr. Bouncely from up front. "Are they behind us?"

"Look!" shrieked Pease. "It's not a sack. It's something else."

118

THE RABBIT'S UMBRELLA

Mr. Bouncely looked over his shoulder and was immediately sorry he had. He yelled out, "Heavens! It's a monster! Shoot him with your gub, Pease—I mean your gat. Blug him."

"I can't plug him," shouted Pease from the third cart. "The gat's rusted."

"Then hit him on the head with the flapjack."

"We haven't a blackjack," shouted Punch.

Mr. Bouncely shouted. He shouted nothing in particular, just shouted, and as he twisted the wheel the car and the three carts tore onto the smooth incline of Willow Street, dipping swiftly through the shadowy trees into Adams.

SEVEN

YOUNG BOY SITTING ON EDGE OF LARGE ARMCHAIR: *My, oh my, that was a noisy chapter. And an exciting one.*

Yes, and exhausting if read aloud with great gusto and feeling, as it should be—reading the frightening bits with the lights low and the fire snapping, and acting out the robbers sneaking through the Montague house and Mr. Bouncely driving Peter's little one-seater. And shouting out Lump's great cry—that's important. In fact, after Lump's yell I don't think I have any vocal cords left. Can you hear me?

YOUNG BOY: *Oh yes.*

Well, regardless, I'm exhausted, and I'd just as soon continue this book some other time, perhaps next month.

YOUNG BOY: *Nonsense, nonsense. Did the rabbit with the umbrella hear the cry? And what about Doctor Trimble, Officer Delaney, and Mr. Otway?*

Yes, they did. But if you don't mind, we'll skip the excitement for the moment until I get my breath back after that last chapter. I should like to give you a relaxing description of scenery, if I may; namely Willow

Hill, where all this breath-taking action is going on.

YOUNG BOY: *You won't be too long with the description, will you?*

Just a few lines. Just enough to describe the steepness of Willow Street as it ducks down through the trees to the outskirts of Adams. Lining the road, chestnut trees are mixed in with the willows, and their big mahogany-colored nuts, swayed loose by the wind or squirrels, whistle down and bounce, *blop*, against the macadam road. Down the hill they bounce, *blop-blop-blop*, and, if they stay clear of the ditches and the scurrying dogs, they *blop-blop* right through the outskirts of Adams into the town square and *thunk* up against Officer Delaney's white traffic box.

You'll see if you look at the map in front of the book that Willow Street continues through the town across the railroad tracks, where it mounts steeply up to the country club, with its golf course, swimming pool, and tennis courts. Across the tracks the willows and the chestnut trees give way to the rolling fairways of the golf course, but although there are no chestnuts to bounce into Adams, often, especially when Doctor Trimble is on the course, there are golf balls. Doctor Trimble approaches a golf ball with the determination and stroke of a farmer hacking at a weed, and occasionally he lifts a ball onto Willow Street.

There it bounces down to the railroad tracks, into the town square, and *thunks* up against Officer Delaney's white traffic box, catching him from the rear.

YOUNG BOY: *Have you recovered your breath yet?*

I suppose so.

YOUNG BOY: *What about Officer Delaney, Mr. Otway, and Doctor Trimble?*

Well, Mr. Otway had parked the streetcar at the end of the line up on top of Willow Hill, overlooking the moonlit valleys. In this lovely setting, a slight wind sifting through the trees above them, Dr. Trimble was telling a story about himself. Officer Delaney and Mr. Otway, sitting forward, were listening intently.

"So I picked up the kangaroo by the tail," Dr. Trimble was saying, "and threw it with all my might at Mr. Bones. What should that scoundrel with the knife in his teeth do but pluck that kangaroo out of the air as if it were a powder puff and hurl it back, knocking me flat on my back in the desert sand, completely at his mercy. 'Well, Mr. Bones,' I said, watching him take the knife from his teeth, 'you're as accurate a shot with a kangaroo as I've ever seen.' "

At this moment Lump's cry slammed up the hill, shivering the moonlight around them.

"What was that?" shouted Officer Delaney.

"What was that?" echoed Mr. Otway.

"I said, 'You're an accurate shot with a kangaroo, Mr. Bones,'" repeated Dr. Trimble, who didn't like to be interrupted.

"It comes from down the hill," whispered Officer Delaney in awe as the cry shattered the night air again. "Come on, Mr. Otway, Doctor Trimble—into the streetcar and we'll see what it is."

"What nonsense," protested Dr. Trimble as he was pushed aboard. "Owls," he said. "Just an owl or two out there in the forest, nothing more." As the streetcar picked up speed down Willow Street he attempted to continue the story of Mr. Bones and the kangaroo. "Well," he said. "Mr. Bones he looked at me and said, 'Admiral Appleton' (which was the name I was traveling under at the time), 'Admiral Appleton, you may think I'm accurate with a kangaroo but wait till you see what I can do with a knife—'"

"Look! Look there!" shouted Mr. Otway and Officer Delaney from the controls. Dr. Trimble puffed angrily, but he looked out the front window. When he saw in the moonlight what was hurtling down Willow Street in front of them he forgot Mr. Bones and the kangaroo. "Why, it's Mr. Montague's remarkable giant panda," he called out excitedly. "Look at him in the first cart." For there, streaking down the

hill toward Adams, were the three robbers and Lump.

"It looks like the Bouncely gang," called out Officer Delaney. "Look at that bag of bones in the last cart; that'll be Pease surer'n shooting. But what's that in the first cart?" he shouted, he face pink with excitement. "It's a bear! They're stealing a bear from the zoo, that's it, they're stealing a bear from our zoo."

Mr. Otway tried to calm him by mentioning that Adams didn't have a zoo and never had had a zoo, and that the creature was Mr. Montague's new dog. He knew because he'd helped to push it up the driveway that afternoon. But Officer Delaney was not to be dissuaded. "It's a bear from our zoo," he insisted, wildly ringing the bell overhead as the streetcar plunged down Willow Street after the fleeing robbers.

"It looks like a bear all right," shouted Dr. Trimble above the bell's clatter and the roar of the wheels beneath them. "It's Mr. Montague's giant panda, straight from the Himalayas." He was almost as excited as Mr. Otway was. "Pile on the speed," he cried. "Pile on more sail."

Then suddenly, as Dr. Trimble capered about behind Officer Delaney and Mr. Otway, shouting orders, he stopped and peered through a side window. "Look there," he called, pointing down at the big patch of yellow light framed against the passing scenery. "It's the rabbit with the umbrella. Look at him down there, running alongside, his ears straight back in the wind."

But Mr. Otway and Officer Delaney were too busy at the controls to turn to look.

YOUNG BOY: *Did the robbers see the rabbit with the umbrella?*

Oh my, no, they were much too concerned with their plight. In the back cart Pease heard the bell, looked over his shoulder, and saw the streetcar bearing down on them like a locomotive. "Punch!" he shouted. "Look!"

And Punch, in the second cart, where he had been staring with horror at Lump's broad back in the first cart, looked over *his* shoulder and his eyes grew as big as Ping-pong balls. "Mr. Bouncely!" he shouted. "Look!"

Up in the one-seater Mr. Bouncely was doing his best. His hair rumpled by the wind, his body shaken by the piston speed of the whirling pedals beneath his feet, he kept his hands clenched hard on the steering wheel and his eyes on the road in front. At Punch's shout he turned, and for the second time that night he was sorry he'd done so as he looked past Lump and saw the streetcar. A cry almost as shattering as Lump's escaped his lips as he turned back to his driving.

The hill dips so sharply into Adams that in the streetcar behind the runaways Mr. Otway had to apply his brakes. Mr. Bouncely, who would have given almost anything to be able to do the same, was of course without brakes; but he noticed with some satisfaction that because of their speed they began to draw away from the streetcar.

At the noise coming down Willow Street the squirrels and chipmunks peered out from behind their stone walls and the annoyed crows looked down from the trees overhead. Their eyes didn't become as large as Ping-pong balls, but as large with astonishment as very small black peas.

First, squeezed into a toy car and three Flying Express carts, came the robbers and a dog that looked the size of an elephant; then came the streetcar, its bell clanging, and swaying from side to side in its speed; then, some distance behind, came a man dressed in pajamas and bedroom slippers. (It was Mr. Montague of course, who, after realizing that the burglars had removed his son's car and dog, had felt that he ought to chase them, and was doing so, the bedroom slippers flapping about his feet.) Finally, as a sort of caboose to this whole procession, a solitary chestnut suddenly detached itself from a bough high overhead and plunked hard against the macadam road and started bouncing in big hops after Mr. Montague, *blop-blop-blop*, toward the center of town.

The first ones to get to the town square were the

robbers. They went by Officer Delaney's traffic box well ahead of the others, moving at considerable speed. But their momentum began to die as they crossed the railroad tracks and headed toward the country club. Pease and Punch, who had shouted, "Slower, Mr. Bouncely, slower!" on the way down Willow Street, now shouted, "Faster, Mr. Bouncely, faster!" Mr. Bouncely did his best. When he was able to get his feet on the whirling pedals he strained to keep them moving. But the slope of the hill proved too much, and just opposite Mrs. Phipps's house they came to a stop.

Up in her house Mrs. Phipps heard the commotion, switched on her light, and went to the window. "Ye gods and little fishes," she whispered as she saw the trainload of robbers below. They were a sinister sight under the big moon—not Chinese tea merchants at all, but the ghosts from the secluded lane where she had put her Ford into reverse the night before. Dr. Trimble had been quite mistaken. Mrs. Phipps clutched her nightgown tight around her and said, "Do something, Rasputin." But when she looked around she saw only the black tip of Rasputin's nose, peeping from under her footstool.

Down in the street Mr. Bouncely saw Mrs. Phipps's light go on. "Get me out of this thing," he shouted. "We'll make a break for the fields."

THE RABBIT'S UMBRELLA

But just as Pease and Punch started to climb down from their carts, Mr. Bouncely lifted his feet from the pedals, and immediately the carts and the car began to slide backward down the hill.

"Stop!" cried Punch, Pease, and Mr. Bouncely. But Mr. Bouncely couldn't get his feet on the whirling pedals, and with Pease suddenly in the lead the three carts and the car sped swiftly toward the town square. "Steer it, Pease!" shouted Mr. Bouncely frantically over his shoulder. But Pease of course had nothing in his cart but his long bony knees and the huge Webley-Vickers revolver in his lap; besides, he was faced in the wrong direction.

They passed the streetcar at the railroad tracks. For a second it looked as if the two would collide, and Mr. Bouncely lifted his hands from the steering wheel and clapped them to his eyes. But in the last few feet the robber train swerved, and thundered on across the railroad tracks into town.

They finally came to a stop next to Officer Delaney's traffic box in the deserted square. Up the hill beyond the railroad tracks the robbers could hear the streetcar bell start to clang again. "Get me out of here," shouted Mr. Bouncely for the second time, "and we'll make a break for the fields."

Pease and Punch jumped down from their carts and

with great effort they managed to pry Mr. Bouncely loose from his car. But as they stood rubbing their cramped limbs, Lump, snuffling slightly, gingerly put a foot down from his cart and stepped into the square.

The three robbers bunched together in a tight knot and retreated toward the town-hall steps. "He's going to attack us," whispered Mr. Bouncely. "Flast him with the pun, Pease," he ordered. "Quick!"

"Yes, blast him with the gun," Punch repeated.

Pease took out the enormous Webley-Vickers. "It doesn't work," he said as he waved it nervously in front of him. "Bang!" he croaked weakly in desperation. "Bang! bang!"

Lump sat down and looked at them, then rose again
and came forward, his feet plumping softly.

Thus Dr. Trimble, Mr. Otway, and Officer Delaney
found them, the three robbers, huddled together on
the town-hall steps. And, in front of them, sitting with
his tongue lolling, was Lump—not an angry Lump,
mind you, just a Lump who after a long and trying day
hoped finally to find sympathetic friends.

Officer Delaney leaped down the streetcar steps and ran toward them, blowing his whistle. He stopped behind Lump. "Reach," he said. "Reach for the skies."

"What's he talking about?" Mr. Bouncely whispered. "What's he mean?"

"He wants us to put our hands in the air," replied Pease, his arms above his head.

"Whatever for?" asked Mr. Bouncely.

"I'll explain later," Punch whispered to him. "But please, please do it, Mr. Bouncely, or we'll have no end of trouble."

So Mr. Bouncely put his hands above his head.

"Higher," commanded Officer Delaney. "Higher!" —until the robbers' arms were so high it seemed as if the three men were hanging by their fingertips from a window sill high above the ground.

"It's kind of like gym exercises." Mr. Bouncely giggled.

"Quiet!" insisted Officer Delaney. Suddenly, in the silence which followed, the sounds of running footsteps came drifting into the town square from the direction of Willow Hill.

"What's that?" whispered Officer Delaney uneasily, as all heads turned.

The footsteps came closer, unearthly padding sounds, echoing in the square.

"Could it be another robber?" suggested Mr. Otway in a frightened voice.

"A robber!" shouted Mr. Bouncely.

"Nonsense," said Dr. Trimble, trying to calm the group. "It's just the rabbit with the umbrella. Wait and see."

But it wasn't the rabbit. There came padding into the square—breathing hard, his arms pumping wearily, and the look on his face of a man doomed to run nowhere forever—a man dressed in pajamas, with a pair of bedroom slippers flapping about his feet.

"Why, it's Mr. Montague," said Mr. Otway, stepping forward to meet him. "Look there, Mr. Montague," he called. "Your dog, that thing we pushed up the driveway this afternoon, caught them." He pointed to the robbers bunched together on the town-hall steps.

"Yes, that giant panda of yours did a fine job," agreed Dr. Trimble.

"Yes sir, Mr. Montague, a fine job," echoed Officer Delaney.

"I see," replied Mr. Montague vaguely. He still wasn't sure what he was doing in the town square in pajamas and bedroom slippers.

He stood and watched the robbers being led away by Officer Delaney; then he whistled softly for Lump and slowly began to walk back up Willow Street. At his

133

side the big dog padded softly along. The night was peaceful, the moon shining full above them, a light wind slowly rocking the branches where the crows once more put their heads beneath their black wings and tried to settle down for a night's rest.

Mr. Montague's wife was waiting up for him. She called from the living room as he came in the front door, "What on earth has happened? What was all that commotion in the garden, and all that yelling down the hill?"

"I don't honestly know," Mr. Montague replied wearily. "I've been running very hard through the night and I'm not sure why." He swayed in the doorway. "I'm very tired," he said. "Perhaps tomorrow we'll find out what tonight was all about." And with that, Mr. Montague went up to bed.

EIGHT

Nobody found out what had really happened until the robbers were brought to trial in the town hall.

The day after all the excitement the people of Adams collected on the street corners, in Mr. Tompkins' drugstore, and on the steps of the town hall, and discussed the events of the night before in high-pitched voices. Wanting to find out what had happened, many of them clustered so thickly around Officer Delaney's white traffic box that Officer Delaney's face grew very red and he shouted, "You're cluttering up my traffic jam! Go and ask Mr. Otway what happened."

And so they trooped off through the traffic jam to the streetcar, becalmed as usual above a motionless sea of car tops, and climbed aboard. "What happened, Mr. Otway?" they asked. Mr. Otway scratched his long chin. "I'm not sure that I rightly know," he finally answered. "You'd better ask Doctor Trimble."

Dr. Trimble was quite sure in his own mind what had gone on the night before, and in Mr. Tompkins' drugstore, surrounded by a large crowd of people, he told such a bloodcurdling tale that the townspeople left him, shaking their heads and feeling fortunate they hadn't been murdered in their beds.

"The Flouncely gang," cried Dr. Trimble, getting the name wrong, "were armed to the teeth. They had one of the biggest pistols I've ever laid my eyes on, so big you would have thought it would take three men to lift it. A ferocious and notorious crew of desperadoes, the Flouncely gang."

A voice broke in from the edge of the circle. "But these were the people I saw on my secluded lane. You told me at the tea party that they were Chinese tea merchants," said Mrs. Phipps.

Eyes turned and stared at her. Dr. Trimble looked at her for a long time, almost sorrowfully, and finally he said gently, "No, ma'am, I'm afraid I don't know what you're talking about. It was the Flouncely gang." Mrs. Phipps suddenly felt she hadn't ever said anything sillier in her life.

But she hadn't much time to feel uncomfortable. With a great swish of his cane Dr. Trimble continued. "And, my friends," he cried, "the notorious Flouncely gang tried to steal the most valuable piece of property in Adams County—Mr. Henry Montague's giant panda, straight from the bamboo forests of the Himalayas." The townspeople sucked in their breath in awe.

136

"The gang arrived," Dr. Trimble went on, "at Mr. Montague's house in a high-powered midget racer—three large trailers attached behind—in which to cart away the loot. In the dead of night they arrived and they would have got away scot-free with the panda if it hadn't been . . ." And Dr. Trimble described the chase down Willow Street, the calm of Mr. Otway as he piloted the streetcar after the fleeing robbers as if it were the sort of thing he did every night, the bravery of Officer Delaney and of Mr. Montague's giant panda, who, just when things were going very badly, stepped in and captured the robbers on the steps of the town hall.

Few people, except for very small boys and their dogs, seriously believed Dr. Trimble, but they listened intently and watched him caper about among the tables of Tompkins' drugstore, striking viciously at the air with his cane. When his performance was over, and Dr. Trimble had taken his bow and started in again for the benefit of newcomers, the townspeople left the drugstore and journeyed up Willow Street to see Mr. Montague's giant panda.

It wasn't a panda, of course, only Lump; but the townspeople, except for very small boys and their dogs, hadn't really expected to find a panda so they weren't too disappointed. They gawked over the gate and walked through the garden, chatting with Mr. Montague and watching Peter play with the dog.

Mr. Montague's bones still ached, but he walked stiff-legged in the garden, considerably cheered about the state of the world. He still had no idea what had really happened the night before, but as he looked around him he saw people more or less pleased with life.

His wife was happy. She felt better about Lump and began to look upon him with sympathy. She was no longer concerned that the dog padding heavily through the house wasn't a poodle called Minnehaha, but was, instead, whatever breed of dog Lump was. And she thought how much nicer it was to have one's pet called "brave," rather than "divine" or "charming."

During breakfast Lump had come in and had sat heavily down in the corner of the dining room. "Lump," she called. The dog looked at her, rose to his feet, and shambled obediently toward her, his big paws hitting the carpet, *plump-plump-plump,* as he came. "Here," said Mrs. Montague when the dog stood before her. "Take this, and *carefully,* please." And she gingerly offered Lump a piece of toast from her plate. The dog's head lowered; his snuffling filled the room as his large black nose bent to her hand. With the delicacy of an elephant's trunk accepting a peanut from a child, Lump's tongue unrolled and gathered up the toast. "How very nice!" cried Mrs. Montague as she reached for more toast. She looked at the dog affectionately and, deciding right then and there to try another tea party the very next Saturday afternoon, she went out to the kitchen to tell the cook.

Peter too was happy that morning, though when he had awakened he remembered that Lump was to be returned to Mr. Perkins' pet shop and that in protest he'd promised himself not to eat or talk for a month. But the odor of pancakes had come drifting in under the bedroom door and, besides, Peter noticed so many people wandering in the garden that he felt he must know what was going on. So he stayed in his room for a while, just as a gesture—pulling at the ring in his elephant to make it squeak—and then he went down to breakfast. There he found that Lump was a hero and, what's more, was being fed toast by his mother. The only thing that caused Peter unhappiness for the rest of the day, as he romped with Lump, was that he'd slept through the commotion the night before and missed all the excitement.

YOUNG BOY: *How about the three robbers? They couldn't have been very happy, being stuck away in jail.*

On the contrary, they were delighted. They enjoyed jail enormously. They had their first good night's sleep in a long time, free of the awful sounds that had terrified them in their years as robbers, such as the shouts of owls and the unsoothing songs droned by death-watch beetles. Three excellent meals a day were served them. Punch purred all day long in contentment, like a fat cat, and even Pease put weight on his long skeleton-like body.

Many visitors came to see them—the curious and, especially, Dr. Trimble, Mr. Otway, and Officer Delaney. Dr. Trimble was anxious to find out if any of the Bouncely gang knew the notorious bandits he had met during his travels around the world.

"You know Mr. Bones, I presume?" he asked Mr.

Bouncely. "As accurate a shot with a kangaroo as I've ever seen—just as if he were hurling a boomerang."

"I don't believe so," replied Mr. Bouncely.

"Or Sam Beebee-Eyes McGillicutty, the pickpocket from Dublin who left his visiting card in place of the wallets he lifted?"

"No," said Mr. Bouncely. "I don't know him either."

"Surely Guts Lonigan," Dr. Trimble insisted, "the Bengalese pirate who made himself a knife so long it wouldn't fit in a sheath; and he's had to carry it naked in his hand for the last twenty years."

"No, I don't know Guts Lonigan," Mr. Bouncely answered, beginning to tremble slightly. "Nor do I know Sam Beebee-Eyes McGillicutty, or even Mr.

Bones. I don't want to. They sound like wretched people."

Dr. Trimble was surprised to hear this, for, as you know, there is supposed to be honor among thieves. But then Mr. Bouncely told him of the Bouncely gang's career, that for one reason or another they'd never managed a successful robbery, and Dr. Trimble quickly realized that the three robbers weren't the ferocious monsters he'd described in Mr. Tompkins' drugstore. He was disturbed about this and, to make amends, he offered his services as lawyer for Pease, Punch, and Mr. Bouncely at their trial.

"Why, we'd be delighted," said Mr. Bouncely, and they solemnly shook hands.

But Dr. Trimble spent so little time in preparing their case that the three robbers began to worry. He came often to the little jail, but he spent his visits frightening Pease, Punch, and Mr. Bouncely—and often Mr. Otway and Officer Delaney, who'd dropped in to pass the time of day—with tales of the famous criminals he had met on his world travels. There were not only Mr. Bones, Sam Beebee-Eyes McGillicutty, and Guts Lonigan, but others—a man called TWO-STORY SMITH, a circus giant who sneaked expensive watches off the wrists of other circus giants and could reach in second-story windows without the aid of a ladder, and a remark-

able criminal called Greasy-Thumb Watkins, who was supposed to have stolen a Long Island Railroad locomotive. When Dr. Trimble wasn't telling about these he held his head in his hands, trying to remember others and their exploits.

During these short silences—while the five fidgeted on their seats, hoping that Dr. Trimble's memory would fail him and that he'd find something less terrifying to discuss—Mr. Otway occasionally would try to start a conversation. "I fell to thinking the other day," he'd say, looking mournfully into the palm of his hand, "about the streetcar—"

"Tiny-Toed Kelley!" Dr. Trimble would shout suddenly. "He robs burglars, not to give the stolen property back to the rightful owner, but to keep for himself."

Mr. Bouncely replied that it was least likely that, among all the criminals Dr. Trimble had described, the Bouncely gang had run into Tiny-Toed Kelley. "He would have starved," said Mr. Bouncely, "waiting around for us to steal something he in turn could burgle from us."

Eventually, though, Mr. Otway found an opportunity during one of the short periods of silence to tell the robbers that the town streetcar was to have its wheels removed and be turned into a Harry's Diner. "Sometime next week," he said, "the town will no longer have its streetcar."

"How curious," said Mr. Bouncely. "Whatever is wrong with the townspeople?"

"Apparently they would rather eat than ride," explained Officer Delaney.

Punch, lolling comfortably in his chair, said he could certainly understand how the townspeople felt, and he drummed his fingers up against the tightening curve of his waistcoat.

"Well then," suggested Mr. Bouncely. "If the mayor's council is so anxious to turn the streetcar into a restaurant, why not let them? But have it a traveling diner. We'll install a little kitchen and serve at mealtimes. Between meals the streetcar can continue its regular runs."

Mr. Otway scratched his head. "It seems a good idea to me," he said.

"An excellent idea!" exclaimed Officer Delaney, his neck muscles bulging with excitement.

"I'd like to volunteer for the position of cook," said Punch eagerly. "I've learned in the past years to cook under difficult conditions—in other people's houses on stoves I haven't seen before. I've learned to roast chickens and bake cakes in the dark, and to mix a salad dressing while trying to open a safe. A streetcar kitchen should be easy after my training. I'm sure I could cook a soufflé while coming full speed down Willow Street."

Mr. Otway was impressed. "As the operator of the streetcar," he said, "I think I'm in a position to say that you're hired."

"One moment," said Officer Delaney gloomily.

145

"There's no guarantee that Mr. Bouncely, Punch, and Pease aren't going to be sent to jail for a long time. Doctor Trimble will have to plead a wonderful case for them; after all, burglary is a very serious crime." He looked at Dr. Trimble. "What do you think their chances are, Doctor?"

Dr. Trimble raised his head from his hands. "To my regret," he said, "I can only remember twenty worthy criminals. Not another seems to come to mind."

Officer Delaney was exasperated. "Listen," he said. "You've got to spend more time in thinking how to plead our friends' case. If we can get them set free we'll have a chance to save the streetcar."

"You mustn't worry," said Dr. Trimble soothingly. "Not only am I thinking hard, but I'm in constant consultation with the rabbit with the umbrella."

At this Mr. Bouncely, Pease, Punch, Officer Delaney, and Mr. Otway looked at one another and shook their heads sadly.

The trial was held three days after the attempted robbery. The courtroom was packed with excited townspeople. A judge from Dover came down to hear the case; he sat high on his bench, folding and unfolding his hands in his lap. Officer Delaney and Mr. Otway sat in the back of the courtroom, and they were worried.

"He looks tough," whispered Officer Delaney. "I don't think we've got a chance."

Mr. Bouncely, Pease, and Punch were just as solemn. When Dr. Trimble arrived, bustling down the aisle with a leather briefcase, he tried to cheer them up. "Don't worry about a thing," he said. But Mr. Bouncely happened to notice that Dr. Trimble's briefcase, lying open on the table in front of him, was empty; there was not so much as a scrap of paper in it.

The judge called the court to order. From the first the robbers' case looked hopeless. They *had* entered Mr. Montague's house, they *had* stolen an animal belonging to Mr. Montague—also one automobile (miniature) and three carts—and those were the facts of the case. And no matter how you turned and twisted them, the facts were indisputable. Witness after witness was called to the stand, and not once did Dr. Trimble challenge one. It looked as if he had given up the case and would make no effort to save the Bouncely gang from the severe sentence that the judge was most likely figuring out with a scratchpad and pencil as he sat on his bench high above them.

Finally the prosecuting attorney made his final remarks, summing up the case against the robbers, and the judge nodded his head and looked down at Dr. Trimble. "The defense has been very silent," he said.

"Does the defense counsel have anything at all to say?"

Dr. Trimble stood up. "Well, I should have mentioned right at the beginning," he said, "that the three defendants plead guilty, and there wasn't much need in calling up that string of witnesses to prove a robbery which they readily admit to having committed."

"The defense, in that case," said the judge angrily, "has wasted a great deal of my time."

"On the contrary," replied Dr. Trimble. "*I* didn't call all those people up to the witness stand to drone on about something we already know."

The judge from Dover stood up and pulled his robes around him. "If the counsel for the defense has nothing more to say on behalf of the prisoners he will sit down and I shall pass the severe sentence that I've been figuring out up here with my scratchpad and pencil."

Dr. Trimble paused a full minute while the courtroom waited breathlessly. Then he tapped his pencil on the table and said, "No, I have nothing to say on behalf of the prisoners. But I do have a warning for the citizens of Adams."

He stood up and struck a theatrical pose before the robbers. "These men," he said, pointing at them, "are amateurs, rank amateurs. Come to think of it, they're worse than amateurs. In their years as robbers they've never managed to steal *anything* very much. They are, in short," he went on, "a disgrace to the entire profession. If you send them to prison," he cried to the judge, "you accuse them of being robbers, and that news, your Honor, would so infuriate the respected members of the profession that they'd descend on this town in droves to show us what robbery is really about.

"And I'll tell you what kind of people would arrive, following the news.

"They'd come in the dead of night, the town asleep and helpless before them, on a train stolen for the occasion by the notorious Greasy-Thumb Watkins. Back in the coaches during the journey the most desperate criminals in the country would be busily sharpening their knives, blunting their blunt instruments, lighting fuses, corking up their poison capsules, and I don't know what-all.

"And these criminals—who are they? Well, I'll tell you.

"Guts Lonigan, with a knife so long he can't stick it in a sheath; Sam Beebee-Eyes McGillicutty, limbering up his fingers on a rubber ball to keep them nimble for picking pockets; the terrible Mr. Bones, itching to pick up something like a lawnmower and throw it at somebody; TWO-STORY SMITH, the circus giant, curled up in his seat like a length of hawser; and, capering about unseen on the back platform of Greasy-Thumb Watkins' train, Tiny-Toed Kelley, rubbing his hands together and looking forward to burgling the burglars.

"These would be the people," cried Dr. Trimble. "And more besides."

And though there was a small scream of protest from Mrs. Phipps, sitting at the back of the courtroom, Dr.

Trimble went into the case histories of these dangerous criminals in great detail. It was all so frightening that the judge's hands stopped unfolding and folding in his lap and he looked down with wide eyes at Dr. Trimble.

Dr. Trimble's voice suddenly became low, sincere, and rich. "These criminals, considering it the grossest sort of insult to be classed in the same company as these misfit amateurs, the Bouncely gang, would flood through this town with cutlasses in their teeth and pistols at the ready. I assure you," he announced to the judge from Dover, "there'd be quite enough of them to overflow into your home town up the railroad line." And with this Dr. Trimble sat down.

The courtroom was breathless. "Well," said the judge nervously. His pencil was poised above the scratchpad. He put the pencil down and cupped his chin in his hands. "Well," he said again, "under these circumstances I think it might be dangerous to keep the three defendants in jail even as much as one more night." He stood up and started for the door. "Let us hope they become decent citizens," he called over his shoulder as he scurried from the courtroom.

A wild sigh of relief went up from the onlookers, and amidst applause and handshakes Mr. Bouncely, Pease, and Punch walked out of the courtroom, free men.

THE RABBIT'S UMBRELLA

YOUNG BOY: *Did the twenty terrible robbers come to Adams anyway—in Greasy-Thumb Watkins' train?*

No they didn't.

YOUNG BOY: *I think that's too bad.*

You ask too much of me. I myself am delighted that the judge from Dover was impressed as he was by the logic of Doctor Trimble's speech, and didn't put the robbers in jail.

YOUNG BOY: *Did anyone from the town ever run into the twenty terrible robbers?*

No, not even Pease, Punch, and Mr. Bouncely. Doctor Trimble's description of professional criminals worried them as much as it did the judge from Dover. The three robbers weren't anxious to leave Adams. They had no wish to run into the terrible Mr. Bones, TWO-STORY SMITH, or any of the others who might have heard that they had disgraced the profession and who might have decided to take it out on them personally.

So Pease, Punch, and Mr. Bouncely settled down in Adams and became what the judge from Dover hoped they'd become—highly respected and decent citizens. Their first week they set to work with Officer Delaney, Mr. Otway, and Doctor Trimble and installed the little kitchen on the streetcar. They ran a pipe up through

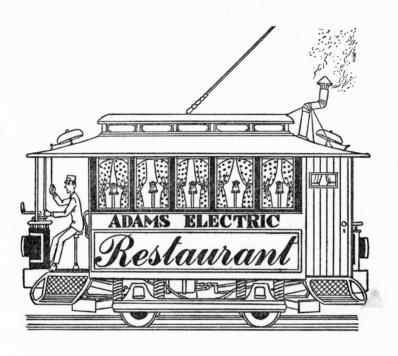

the roof for the galley stove and between the seats they
set up tables.

At first the townspeople came to the transformed
streetcar out of curiosity. But when they tasted Punch's
cooking they came back again and again. Breakfast was
served down by the Montague thimble factory, and for
lunch and dinner you could board the streetcar in the
town square and, after the journey up Willow Hill,
have your meal while looking down across the valleys
of Adams County.

The streetcar meals became so popular that you had to arrive early to get a table, and in the meetings of the town council the advisability of putting the wheels back on the *other* streetcar was often discussed.

So you can see that when the bright Saturday afternoon of Mrs. Montague's second tea party arrived—the one she had planned to show off the brave Lump—things had quieted down in Adams. The nights were calm and the crows roosted comfortably on their pine-tree perches until the dawn came, bringing the bright long days.

The tea party itself was a great success. Even Mrs. Phipps stared at Lump in awe, and finally she fed him a piece of cinnamon toast. Lump didn't perform any tricks, but he sat around, lifting a foot occasionally to dislodge an itch, and he thought life was just fine. So did everybody else.

Well, now that we've been through a hectic week in Adams, I think you, Young Boy, and I ought to leave Mrs. Montague's tea party and wander toward town under the trees of Willow Street. We mustn't forget to wave at Mr. Otway at the controls of the streetcar as it passes, and to Punch in his chef's hat, working at the little galley stove. Of course we ought to stop and chat with Officer Delaney in his traffic box, and we'll just

THE RABBIT'S UMBRELLA

have time to pay a short visit to Mr. Perkins' pet shop.

Now, Young Boy, if you'll just carry that box of pink-eyed mice and the tin pail full of bullfrogs that Mr. Perkins has managed to sell us, we'll get down to the station and catch a train for San Francisco, Chicago, Baltimore, or wherever it was we came from.

YOUNG BOY: *But there are more things I want to know. I want to know about the rabbit with the umbrella.*

Well, in that case we'll have to have an epilogue.

YOUNG BOY: *What is an epilogue?*

It's used to explain what hasn't been explained, to tie up loose strings, and generally to tidy up the book. Turn the page and you'll see.

EPILOGUE

You want to know about the rabbit with the umbrella.
Doctor Trimble would be the one to explain it to you.
He has not only seen the rabbits but also chipmunks
with parasols and sun helmets and squirrels with small
pianos in their houses, and he has seen the mice skate
on the frozen lakes in winter. He has seen so many um-
brella-carrying rabbits that if he were writing this epilogue it would be as long as the book itself. He told me
once he had seen a whole field full of rabbits opening
and shutting their umbrellas after a summer rainstorm,
the drops shaken off sparkling like diamonds in the
new sun.

I have never seen one myself, though I think I saw
one smelling a petunia when I was a boy your age, playing in my great-grandfather's garden. But Doctor Trimble tells me the reason dogs roll their tongues out and
laugh is that they recall suddenly how funny a rabbit
looks, leaping through a hedgerow with an open umbrella bouncing above him. And I have seen dogs laugh
suddenly for no apparent reason at all. I am glad to

156

know why. Doctor Trimble explains that the rabbits cut holes in the umbrella for their ears to stick through, and you can see why that should be amusing to anyone —especially dogs, who are ready to laugh at anything.

And where are these rabbits to be found? On the other side of mirrors and trees, skipping about behind closed doors, perched on the chair immediately behind you, and so quick-moving that no matter how fast you turn around you can't quite see them. They are to be found behind the closed eyelids of sleeping children and hopping through the dreams of tabby cats; and as they run across the dark fields at night the heads of cattle turn calmly to watch them hurry by. Cattle are surprised at nothing, and the rabbits don't mind being seen by them. But it would never do to be seen by a human being (except one like Doctor Trimble) and that is why the rabbits are so shy. For grown persons would shout, "Great Heavens, a rabbit with an umbrella!" and clasp their hands over their eyes and rush headlong through the forest, bumping into trees and falling into ponds, arriving finally at a police station, where it would be embarrassing, very embarrassing, to watch the deepening color of a police sergeant's face when he's told that rabbits with umbrellas run loose in the forests.

And so you will ask why I put a rabbit with an

umbrella into a book mostly about human beings. That would be hard to answer. Doctor Trimble would say that *all* books should have at least three rabbits, at least two dancing camels, and a piano-playing woodchuck; that it spruces a book up to have such curious and mysterious characters in it. Perhaps that's why I put the rabbit in this book. Life is full of mysteries, and it's nice to have a mystery that is a rabbit with an umbrella. This book, like life, is also full of mysteries, and there's no reason why the rabbit with the umbrella, though a mystery himself, shouldn't explain many of them.

Wasn't it the rabbit with the umbrella that discouraged Mrs. Montague's dislike of dogs? And what on earth, for example, prompted Mr. Montague to buy Lump from Mr. Perkins if it wasn't the rabbit, perched lightly on his shoulder? And wasn't it that same rabbit, running full speed down Willow Hill alongside Lump's cart, that whispered to the dog to let out the yell that awakened the entire countryside? And don't you suppose it was the rabbit that whispered in Doctor Trimble's ear, to remind him of the twenty burglars whose mention so terrified the judge from Dover? And what gave Mr. Bouncely the idea of turning the streetcar into a traveling restaurant? Wasn't it the rabbit with the umbrella?

But you can't answer, Young Boy, for it appears

you've fallen asleep in your large armchair. How very odd—falling asleep during an epilogue!

Perhaps, though, you're standing at the edge of a forest in the evening. A storm has passed, leaving the trees heavy with rain, and the forest is noisy as the big raindrops roll off the leaves, hitting the underbrush far below. And look! There's the rabbit, his ears straight up through the holes of his umbrella, watching you carefully. Softly now, don't say a word. There he is, stepping out of the forest and coming toward you, picking his way carefully around the puddles. Are those galoshes he's wearing? Well, I don't know—you can see him so much better than I can.

Good night, Young Boy, good night.

DATE DUE